SYMPHONY

A Novel by

Natasha Simmons

Symphony

ISBN-13: 978-0-9967127-2-9
ISBN-10: 0-9967127-2-0

Published by Thomas Publishing

Thomas | Publishing

To Phil, with love. My gate keeper, my dream weaver, my moon catcher, and smile reflector. Because of you, my dreams are tangible.

N.S.

Symphony

ACKNOWLEDGEMENTS

I am continually thankful for my faithful readers who have waited eagerly for Symphony's story.

Thank you, to Bobbie Thurman, who reads pages willingly to make sure my characters' stories translate in such a way that makes sense to the reader. Your extra pair of eyes, comments, and applause are invaluable.

Symphony

Symphony

Hanging off the edge of reality, dangling just above exquisite surrender ...

Prologue

Dear Diary,

I feel like a page of a book, dog-eared at the corner.

Stuck...

I'm waiting for hands to pick me up, run their fingers over my lines, comprehend me, know my words, and treasure me as their favorite.

Chapter 1

Jacksonville, FL

Orgasms are not created equally.

This was no great epiphany—simply a fact, to anyone who's experienced more than one.

Lives were defined in moments of ecstasy or so it seemed. Symphony sought nor received any life affirmations—at least not today.

Gasping for air as she descended, skin warm, damp, and still pulsing, she was already shelving this particular orgasm with the others that neither left her unsatisfied nor fulfilled and was thinking about the tasks she would have to do at work in the morning.

This—all of this.

The hotel room, Eric, meeting twice a month, and the no attachment rule. It was all a means to an end.

That's not to say that she didn't think Eric was a good lover; he was exceptional, in fact. He made her feel sexy, wanton—completely free. And well, there was always the moment of arrival at the end of it all.

The Arrival.

Symphony

That's what he called it. He always made sure she arrived. Yet somehow, it didn't seem like enough to her.

Just like a car trip, there was more than one way to get to your destination. Sometimes, you took the expressway, sometimes the more scenic route. Sometimes you drove all night along the coast and the beauty of it took your breath away.

And then there were times when you traveled through the mountains, climbing so high, there was no possible way you wouldn't drive off the precarious edge of the cliffs. Somehow, though, you manage not to. All the while, overlooking waves, crashing and breaking on the rocks below.

The drives were necessary to get to a particular destination—necessary to keep the car running at tiptop shape.

They were essential to maintain sanity.

Maintenance.

That's how she would describe their relationship if someone were to ask. If someone wanted to know why there was a standing appointment with this man penciled into her calendar, she would tell them it was simply maintenance.

No one would ask.

There was no one to ask.

Symphony

"Leaving me already?" The muffled voice of a man worked to the verge of exhaustion, came from behind her.

"It's late." The two words spoken softly, an answer and an accusation. She was normally home by now. Their tryst ran long and she still had nearly a forty-five-minute drive home.

Symphony had no complaints except the fact that she would have little sleep. She owned a bakery and had to be up before dawn. She and Eric normally met on Saturday evenings, but couldn't seem to fit it into their schedules this time. He had a conference in Orlando and she a large catering job that required her personal attention. Sunday evening was their only option.

"Symphony." His tone more forceful.

"Yes?" Had he been talking to her?

I said, "Then stay."

"I can't." It was the conversation they always had. This tête-à-tête, back and forth that was expected of two lovers, but didn't really apply to them. They both knew the rules:

No overnights. No personal conversations. No dates and most importantly, no emotional ties.

She didn't date. She'd tried a couple of times after college, with horrific results. She'd ended up having to get a restraining order for Delton Cleveland after two outings to the movies and an afternoon of coffee. It had been a favor to her aunt. The man wouldn't take "no" for an answer and had ended up breaking into her apartment and cutting up all of her clothes.

The second loser was Griffin George. He was friendly enough and they had great conversations. He was a lover of classical music like she was, so they attended the symphony and operas every chance they got. After four months, they'd taken a trip to Miami together. One of her favorite composers was performing. She'd drank more than a bit and found herself opening up to him.

She'd told him that her parents had not been in her life since she was a little girl and that she'd grown up with her aunt. Since he had such a close relationship with his parents, he felt that she was limiting the richness of her life by continuing to shut them out. So, George felt it was his sworn duty to "fix" her. He felt she was too ridged, too closed off, and that this was a direct result of not having her parents in her life.

In her mind, she and George were great friends with common interests, but to him, they were on the road to marriage.

Symphony

One day, after the trip to Miami, he told her he had a surprise for her. They'd met at one of their favorite restaurants. He'd booked a private room and just as the maître d' reached the door to show them into it, Griffin got down on one knee and asked her to marry him. Applause from inside the room made her dazed head snap to stare at the people already in the room. There stood his parents, whom she'd met only once, with ecstatic grins and her aunt looking grim.

Griffin tugged her hand to regain her attention. All traces of moisture left her mouth. She had no idea he had these types of feelings for her. Of course, he'd mentioned once or twice that they were perfect for each other, but she had no idea he felt this way. She'd been about to tell him they needed to talk privately, when she heard a voice from behind her that should've been familiar, but wasn't.

It was her mother.

"I wanted us to start our lives off on a branch of healing and love." He told her on the heels of her mother's arrival.

Eyes blazing, she yanked her hand from his as if he'd burnt her. "How dare you!" Anger choked her, but she managed to regain her composure long enough to voice for the world to hear that she didn't love him, never had, and their friendship was lost, because of his blatant, unsolicited intrusion into her personal life.

Thinking back on those experiences made Symphony thankful for the no-strings arrangement she shared with Eric.

She looked over her shoulder. The line of Eric's back dipped a bit before curving over his beautiful backside—dark chocolate flesh that felt so damn good in her hands. This man had the most gorgeous behind she'd ever seen, she thought. He was like rich European chocolate—fine, delicious, and indulgent.

She lifted a hand to trace the path her eyes had just taken and for just a heartbeat, she thought about staying. Her hand hovered above him, but she brought it back to her side as she slid one leg out of the bed and then the other. She heard his quiet sigh.

This paused her.

"What?" The sour taste of annoyance coated her tongue.

Eric turned to face her. "You never stay."

Still irritated from the thoughts of the likes of Delton and Griffin, her words slipped out without her usual care of placing them just so.

"I'm not here to *stay*!" The retort was too quick—too layered with barbed wire. She knew it, the moment he visibly flinched and the warm after-sex smoke in his voice and eyes quickly turned to ice.

Her feet touched the thin carpet of the hotel room floor, punctuating the ending of something that had been convenient and damn near perfect for her needs. She turned to look at him.

It was time.

More and more she'd noticed him staring at her with a look that scared the hell out of her. She'd seen it in others. They were gone now because of it.

Passion, desire, heat, lust... those looks she could stand and even welcomed, but lately, there had been, not only mutual need in his gaze, which she could handle, but rather, there was expectation and obligation hovering in them—those, she could not handle.

Symphony bent over to snatch her clothes from the floor that had been removed from her so delicately as soon as they'd arrived. She wanted him to get a good view of her naked ass and know what he was messing up.

This was the reason she didn't do relationships. She didn't want to be obligated to anyone, didn't want any expectations other than to meet, have sex, and go their separate ways until it was time to do it all again.

She didn't know how to do anything else.

Symphony

She was human, yes. She wanted the physical connection with someone, craved it in fact, but she didn't know what it felt like to be really touched by anyone.

Not anymore.

Symphony looked back at Eric before she closed the bathroom door to get dressed and leave. She saw exactly where this was going and would move on before he turned into a Griffin George. What she didn't see was the cloud of rage hardening Eric's features as he glared at the closed door.

Chapter 2

8 months later
St. Augustine, FL

On the rare occasions she was forced to interact with the customers, Symphony felt like they looked at her as if she'd pissed in the coffee. However, she knew that what she was actually seeing in their eyes was fear. Fear that she might be in a fouler mood than normal and snatch away the cups of special blend coffee that were strapped to their lips or deny them one of her pastries.

As a business owner, she knew she should be grateful for the patronage, but there seemed to be an almost obsessive quality to her customers' behavior, like that of a junkie and his heroin dealer.

Symphony peered through the little window in the door separating her from them. As usual, the bakery was swarming like ants on a half-eaten donut. It was like this every Monday morning at seven-thirty when her special of the week was served. She was open every day but Sunday—Sundays were for her.

There was definitely a love-hate relationship between her and her customers. She loved to bake for them, but she hated to interact with them or anyone for that matter, outside of her kitchen.

"Is Symphony in today?" She heard a customer ask Marylyn at the counter.

Symphony moved away from the window when she saw one of the regulars approach the register near the door, so she couldn't be seen.

"Yea, she's in the back fighting with the mixer again" Marylyn whispered.

"Is she always like that? Mad at the world I mean?"

"Mmhm, but she's OK when she's in the kitchen as long as everyone does exactly what she wants."

"Well, what in the world is the matter with her? Seems like a woman that could make a puff as delicate as she can, would have a better disposition. Doesn't she ever smile or laugh?" The customer looked at the door to the kitchen then back at Marylyn, waiting on a reply.

Marylyn leaned closer to the woman. "Ian," she began in a hushed tone, "the guy who bakes with her sometimes, said he almost saw her smile once when an order of chocolate she wanted, arrived in perfect condition from some place overseas or somewhere, but then she saw him walk in and she started barking

Symphony

orders at him to prepare it some kind of way." Marylyn waved her hand in the air. "I don't know. I try to stay outta there unless it's life or death or something."

Resting her elbows on the counter, Marylyn looked towards the kitchen door and then back at the woman, "I heard that she'd fallen in love with some guy in college and he left her for a job in New York or somewhere up north." She stood again as if sensing she'd said too much, "You gonna eat here today?" She asked the customer in a more casual tone.

"No, with my luck, this'll be the day she decides to come out and try to stare us down until our heads pop off." The woman's frown disappeared and she gave a tentative smile. "I'll take my order to go, thank you."

Symphony leaned against a counter in the kitchen and sighed. She was glad Marylyn and Stephanie decided to show up for work on time today. She hated to work the counter. The customers were always bubbling with comments about how good her pastries were or asking her how she came up with the ideas for the specials she made every week.

Why couldn't they just enjoy them and leave her out of it? She didn't ask *them* deep probing questions or why they decided to come into her shop.

Symphony

She knew why; they wanted something sweet and delicious to eat.

That's all she cared about.

She was there to bake them something good to eat, not to be their friend, not to be their counselor, not to hear about how their grandkids loved the cookies, and definitely not to be solicited into going out on a date with some guy that was arrogant enough to think he had the key to unlock her heart. Been there; done that.

There was no key.

And the lock was sealed and hardened.

Somewhere her guy was off living his life without her, because she was too afraid of the feelings he'd stirred within her. It didn't matter how many Erics came and went, no guy could ever fill the void that was left when *he* went away.

"One day," he'd said. "One day, when you're ready to admit you love me, I'm going to walk back into your life and let you." He was gone. She hadn't really expected him to leave without a fight.

But he had.

She looked around at what she considered perfection—her kitchen. It was the pulse of her world where she orchestrated perfect concertos in the form of warm decadent bits of heaven.

Symphony

In her kitchen, she had complete control. Her aunt Helen had loved classical music and always worked with it blaring from the overhead speakers of her bakery. It was Helen who had named her Symphony and after working with Aunt Helen since the time she could be trusted to operate the oven, she had grown to love classical music as well. It had also become a staple in Symphony's kitchen when she opened her own bakery after her aunt retired and moved to the coast of South Carolina.

Ovens lined one wall, still warm and breathing cinnamon and orange spice from the morning baking. Her pastry racks stood in stoic ranks along the back with tiny golden mounds of cake that would be prepared for a wedding shower later, and in the center was where she created countless works of art on her stainless steel counters.

Her cookware hung above the counters from walnut wood beams that crossed the ceiling. She could probably bake with her eyes closed without missing a beat and, in fact, she often did. This was where she poured out her soul and opened her heart. In only this place could she express her love.

Symphony thought about what she'd heard Marylyn tell the customer about being in love with a guy who left her.

Symphony

"Terry Phoenix," she voiced in a slow jagged sigh.

It was more than a name.

It was a statement that pressed on her heart like the taunt spring of a mouse trap. He'd loved everything she baked and she knew in her heart that she still baked for him.

Refusing to let Terry occupy her thoughts that morning, though he was always there, she stood and walked towards the current bane of her existence.

She frowned again at the temperamental beast that had been at the very least, a faithful adversary and knew it would have to be replaced soon. In front of the mixer with her feet planted apart and her hands on her hips, she glared at it, almost taunting it to defy her.

Symphony could see her reflection in the mixer. The brown eyes he'd thought were so saucy and beautiful, were now dull and hard. They seemed almost out of place on her tan face that housed a tiny dimple on each side that few people saw, because she no longer felt the need to smile. Auburn flames licked the edges of the net cap—her hair never seemed to be contained. It was how she felt most of the time— reaching out over the edge. Too far out to go back and not free enough to stumble forward.

Symphony

At that moment, she tried to will the corners of her mouth to turn up; her cheeks twitched a little, but she heard talking near the door and thought better of it.

Instead, she flipped the mixer's switch on.

Nothing.

And then off again.

On off, on off, on off—she squeezed and flipped the switch until her fingers hurt. She closed her eyes, turned the mixer on once more and listened for even the smallest hint of life within it.

"Come on you bastard, start!" She had a couple of catering orders she needed to get out. Not today. She didn't need this today. Feeling defeated, she rested her forehead on the mixer. With the back of her hand she slapped away the tear that threatened to burn a path down her cheek.

What was wrong with her today?

She'd been on the verge of tears since she woke up this morning—like some horrid tragedy was looming over her.

The vise in her throat held back the sob that clawed its way up from the dredges of nowhere; she would not, could not let it escape. When her hand was no longer enough to manage the pitiful hot trails of salty treachery, she reached for a towel off the counter and wiped her face until she was sure her smooth golden skin was red and raw.

Her throat betrayed her when a silent sob crept forth, but in her head she heard the sickening sound of steel being pulled apart. With the towel still in her hand she assaulted the mixer with the furry of a World War II fighter jet propeller.

Why had she been so stupid to fall for a guy she couldn't have?

She reached for another towel from the other side of the island counter, jerked it away, and in the process sent ten pounds of an opened bag of flour sailing against the side of the mixer, causing an explosion of the powdery staple.

At that moment, Symphony saw Marylyn walk into the kitchen and freeze. As with any combat soldier in a warzone, she knew when to stand her ground and when to flee a hostile situation. For a few seconds, Marylyn's eyes darted around the kitchen, looked at Symphony covered in flour with towels gripped in both hands, eyes blazing, and before her foot had enough time to hit the floor to complete a step, she moved it back to where it started and eased backwards through the swinging door.

Symphony knew for absolute certainty that she would not be disturbed in her sanctuary again, anytime soon. Marylyn knew when it was time to retreat, Stephanie wouldn't dare, and her two morning helpers Ian and Ricco wouldn't be back for a couple of hours.

Symphony let the towels drop from her hands and fall at her feet. Her eyes followed them. They lay there against the cool surface of the white tiles as if resting from a difficult morning. She wondered what it felt like to lie there and just be—no requirements, no feelings, no nothing. She stared at them and then without disturbing their position, she eased herself down to her knees and laid herself flat between them and tried to just let herself be.

With her arms stretched above her, she pressed her palms flat against the floor feeling the velvety layer of flour beneath. Her cheek, she knew, was caked with the stuff. She just closed her eyes, felt the tile press against her face, cold and hard at first, then warm and pulsing, as if it had a heartbeat.

She listened. Da-dump…da-dump…da-dump…da-dump…. The buttons of her coat pushed against her belly and chest and her nose tickled from the flour she was breathing in. Turning to her back, Symphony brought her arms to lie across her chest.

There it was again; the tightness there as if her heart was strapped between cars pulling from opposite directions.

Symphony

She had loved him for years… hoping.
But Terry had not come back.

Chapter 3

There on the floor with her face half-caked in flour, she remembered the moment she'd first caught a glimpse of him. It had been the last semester of her senior year in college at one of the local schools in St. Augustine, FL. She walked into the library and he was walking out. He held the door open for her, but she was so busy looking at a book in her hand, the courtesy nearly went unacknowledged. Just as he was releasing the door and leaving the threshold, she looked up to give him a perfunctory, "Thank you."

In his eyes she saw a flash of disappointment before they brightened, as he replied, "Anytime."

Something about the way he'd said it, made her watch him walk away. The next day, she returned to the library to finish some research and there he was again, standing in the section that shelved the books she was looking for.

"Hello." He said.

"Hi." She answered without really paying attention to who'd spoken. She was looking down at the slip of paper in her hand and then up again at the row of books lining the shelf.

"Symphony, right?"

Symphony

Looking up at him as if she'd just noticed him standing there, she realized it was the guy that held the door for her the day before. She wondered how he could've possibly known her name. She had few friends, because she spent most of her time studying and the rest working in her aunt's bakery.

Symphony cocked her head to the side and raised her brows. She definitely didn't mind that he knew her name, but was still curious as to how he did. He was about the same complexion as her with wavy black hair that was just long enough for fingers to get tangled in. She wondered if he was of mixed heritage. His eyes were dark brown and framed by the most perfect pair of brows she'd ever seen; black and slick and his smile, she noticed keenly, held the hint of unspoken promises.

She was sure many females considered him handsome, but it was more than that. There was a quiet self-assurance about him that told her that this guy could definitely handle anything she threw out.

Why that thought popped in her head was a mystery. She'd not been interested in anyone at school, yet here she was checking out this stranger.

"Sounds like you're waiting for an answer to a question you already seem to be sure of." She replied to his question about her name.

Symphony

He gave her a slow closed-lipped smile, nodded his head, and continued to a full grin that made little tiny bursts of light, flare in her belly.

That smile, she knew could cause her to submit to any temptation, and she didn't like it one bit. She prided herself on always being in control. She was the maestro that directed the world in which she came in contact. It was a survival instinct.

When she was a little girl, there was so much that she had no control over, that she promised herself she would keep tight reins on her life when she got older. She knew that this guy could cause them to slip from her grip.

Turning her back on him, Symphony faced the books and tried like hell to slow down the drumming in her chest, she selected one, and without looking at him again and without knowing why, she said,

"If you were as smart as you try to appear to be, you would've asked a question you didn't know the answer to." And then she was gone.

It was nearly time for mid-terms before she saw him again in the library sitting with his head lying on the hard wooden table amongst a fort-like wall of books. He looked so cute lying there, vulnerable, and clearly exhausted. She almost sat in the chair next to him, but didn't.

Since that first day she'd seen him at the entrance of the library, she caught glimpses of him seemingly everywhere. Symphony was sure he was getting his business degree, like her, because she saw him on campus near the buildings for the college of business, often. On the few occasions they'd made eye contact, he looked as if he wanted to say something to her, but would turn away and go about his business, leaving Symphony with the tiniest piece of disappointment floating in her middle.

One morning under an angry sky, she turned in the student parking lot nearly on two wheels. She was three minutes from being shut out of Dr. Graham's class.

As soon as the clock clicked 9:00am, he locked the door. "Punctuality has a price," he often said when every eye in class turned to the rattle of the doorknob or the unanswered knock after class had begun.

This was not a day to get locked out; he was giving the review for the final. She'd heard that it was nearly impossible to pass without the notes from the review. Looking up at the groaning darkness, she snatched her backpack from her backseat and prayed she could make it from her car to the building across the courtyard in two and a half minutes. Suddenly, a nauseating sound like the heavens being ripped apart, was the introduction to a fast pounding rain. Nearly blinded by the force and volume of it, she ran to the nearest covering.

Within seconds she was soaked, trying to shield her backpack with her arms and body. Her books were too expense to sacrifice for her hair or clothes, plus her laptop was in it too. Hair plastered to her face and clothes running with water like she was a human faucet, she ducked into an alcove at the back of the student center.

Locked.

It was an emergency exit.

The wind whipped through the little space with jagged fierceness and the rain made it impossible to see a thing. Wondering how long it would last, all hopes of making it to class on time was lost. The weather would not matter to Dr. Graham; he was the Darth Vader of Strategy and Problems in Management—ruthless and inflexible.

Just then, another figure dashed into the alcove and knocked her over causing her to scream, more from surprise than fear.

"Shit! I'm sorry!" She heard, vaguely over the storm.

Symphony

She'd fallen on her hip, saving the backpack, again, from the force of the fall. It was a male voice.

"Damnit Dude! Give a girl a break!" She'd scraped her knuckles on the cement pavement and didn't know whether to soothe it or her hip first. Sliding the backpack away from her, she shook the injured hand and pushed gingerly with the other one to try to get back on her feet. She felt a tug on her arm and let the stranger help her up.

"I'm so sorry. Are you ok? Shit! I didn't even see you. This weather is crazy down here."

She looked up into the face of her assailant. It was the guy from the library. He gave her a tilted smile that seemed to tilt her a bit and she suddenly felt self-conscious of her appearance, although he looked as bedraggled as she felt. Rubbing her hip she stepped cautiously to test out its ability to still support her.

"Are you ok?" He asked, holding is arms open a bit as if he was bracing to catch her if she fell.

"I'll live." She tested out her other limbs. "Do you play football? You tackled me like a pro."

He laughed.

"Where're you from?" She asked.

"What makes you think I'm from somewhere else?"

"Because you said, 'this weather is crazy *down* here.'" She twisted her hair and rivulets flowed to the ground. "All Floridians know that thunder storms often come up out of nowhere." She gave him an expectant look.

He chuckled softly. "That obvious, huh?"

"Yea, plus you're wearing loafers. The norm is some sort of flip flop or sandal…." She waited for his reply. "So?" The wind kicked up pushing a fresh spray of rain on them. The shock of it, snatched her breath away.

They moved farther back into the alcove, but it didn't help much. Lightning lit the part of the sky that they could see and thunder shook the campus with a loud angry growl.

He looked as if a monster was barreling down on them. "Was that thunder?"

"Yea." She looked up at him—amusement and astonishment coated the reply.

"We don't get thunder like that in Massachusetts and after more than three years here, I'm still not used to these thunderstorms."

She nodded her head. "I knew you weren't from here. What brought you all the way to our tiny college?"

He stared at her for a few beats too long. "The beach." He said, flicking a wink at her.

Why her body decided to respond to that little gesture, she had no idea, but it had, and she found herself wanting to get to know this Yankee from Massachusetts. "What part?"

He lifted his hand to wipe water from his forehead and she noticed the watch on his arm. A very nice watch. No college student she knew, wore expensive watches. She wondered what he was really doing in St. Augustine, a tiny little tourist town, when he had access to so many more in New England.

"Oh no." She groaned.

"What's wrong?" he asked.

"I'm missing Professor Graham's review." She sank to the ground and put her hand in her head, not caring that the cement was wet.

He squatted down to her. "I have the notes. I had his class yesterday."

She looked up at him, hopeful. "You do?"

He nodded his head with a triumphant smile. "Yep."

"For Strategy and Problems—"

"...in Management," finishing her statement. He nodded, again. "Yep."

"Where's your cape?"

"What?" Confusion lined his face.

"Your cape, because you just saved the day."

He rolled his eyes at her corny line and helped her up.

"I'm Terry Phoenix, by the way." He said, extending his hand. She shook it. "Why couldn't I have met you four years ago?" He mumbled.

Symphony didn't hear what he'd said. She was too excited about being able to get the notes. She also didn't pay any attention to the sad smile he wore.

They made plans to go over the notes the next afternoon when they were both done with classes for the day. It took nearly two hours. While Symphony copied the notes including any additional explanations Terry gave, she would glance up at him every now and then, and noticed he was doing the same.

Terry Phoenix was from a suburb outside of Boston and wasn't particularly a big fan of higher education. He was expected to work in the family business and was forced to attend college. He'd made a deal with his parents that if he had to go, he would go to school where he could be near the beach and lots of sun, so he'd ended up in Florida.

He was from the upper echelon of society, as she'd figured when she saw the watch. He'd come from a different world than where she lived.

Symphony

They were packing up to leave and Symphony could tell he wanted to say something and had even caught his mouth open to do so a few times. While she sat expectantly, he would either say something about the notes or look away. It was a mixture of being cute and infuriating at the same time.

Oh, the hell with this!

"This is how it's done." She quietly announced, and he lifted his head to look at her.

"Huh?"

"I'm available this Friday night if you want to go out with me. You can pick me up at Helen's Bakery on St. George St. Do you know where that is?"

"Yes." His eyes twinkled.

"I'll be ready at seven. Is that time good for you?

"Yes."

"Will I see you Friday at seven?"

"Yes."

"Small talk is so overrated." She walked away.

He was there that Friday night and most nights, until the end of the semester. Every time they met, she had something special she made just for him and he always said that his special treat was better than the one before it.

Symphony

She loved making things for him, because he always appreciated the skill, time, and heart she put into them. She had never met another person she enjoyed being with so much. They would talk for hours after she finished work, sitting right there in the bakery or on long walks. Occasionally they would go out, but it was the nights in the dim quiet of the bakery that she relished.

One night after they both graduated, he didn't show—which was becoming a bit of a habit. Not that he didn't want to be there, he was traveling around deciding which branch of his family's business he would work, and sometimes he just didn't make it back in time for their evening ritual. She was used to it, but, this time was different, they were supposed to be celebrating a catering job she'd gotten on her own.

The couple getting married hired one company for dinner and her for all the desserts for the wedding, rehearsal dinner, and showers. It was a huge opportunity that was going to make her lots of money and hopefully get her name out there. She wanted people to know that although she worked with her aunt, she had skills of her own.

She walked to the door, pulled the shade back and walked back to a stool at the counter. She did that for about an hour, and then went to the back, grabbed ingredients to make any kind of dough; she didn't care, she just needed to do something with her hands.

She pushed hard on the doughy mound squeezing it out in all directions. She picked it up, slammed it on the counter not caring that she was getting flour all over her clothes and everywhere else, not caring that the dough was getting too hard to be of any good for anything.

She pushed, pounded, and dug her fists into it until the tears being mixed with it were more than she could understand. She felt like someone was scraping the insides of her stomach with an ice cream scoop. She loathed the fact that she had allowed herself to care about someone enough to be disappointed by something they did. She also knew that it was time for them to go their separate ways.

Later that night, Symphony sat up in bed and stared at the phone ringing beside her. She placed her hand on the receiver unable to stop the tears and picked it up.

"Yes?" She tried to make her voice as passive as she could.

"I'm sorry, I got held up out of town."

"That's OK, Aunt Helen had me going over all her books and receipts for her most of the night anyway." She lied.

Symphony

"Symphony, I'm sorry. My phone was dead and I was stuck on the plane."

"Look, Terry, I told you it was fine. We knew it would end someday anyway; might as well be now."

"What're you talking about, Symphony? Ending what?'

"This, Terry, whatever we are. It's time for you to go to your job in New England and I'm trying to establish my own business, here." There was silence for a while before he spoke again.

"Symphony let me come over there so we can talk. We can work this out."

"Terry, I'm already in bed."

"Please, Symphony. I want to see you." There was no way she could deny his piteous tone.

She knew it was useless to talk about it, but she did want to see him. She also knew it would be the last time.

"Ok."

It only took him about twenty minutes to get there and when he knocked softly on the door, her lids slid shut for a moment and she took in a deep shaky breath. Lifting her chin, she walked to the door to say goodbye, in a language they'd never spoken before.

Her auburn hair hung loose, curly, and wild—like he liked it. She wore a black clingy, soft knit nightgown that barely reached her thighs. She put it on, because she knew he would like how it hugged her curves. Ignoring the crash and shards of pain her broken heart was causing, she placed a smile on her face, because she knew he liked it.

Intensity, sharp and frightening greeted her when she opened the door.

Fear, not of him, but of the aftermath of what the night would bring.

He stepped inside, closing the door behind him looking like the businessman he was destined to be. She knew he'd probably left his coat and tie in his car, but it didn't matter, he wore the position in his presence.

They lived a lifetime looking into each other. A lifetime, seconds, and not at all. She didn't know who reached for who first, she just knew they ended up in a tangled fury. They didn't seem to know where to touch, taste, or kiss. She kissed his eyelids, his sexy brows, his cheeks, his forehead, his mouth.

His mouth.

The mouth that had whispered all the things that makes a girl feel pretty. All the things that makes her brave. All the things that makes her confident. All the things that makes her fall in love.

Symphony

Her heart slowed and she could hear the echoes of the beats vibrating against her throat. She tried to tame the madness of the kiss and savor him. She wanted to remember every line and indention of his lips. She wanted to remember the curves of his tongue and how it tasted as it threaded around hers. She wanted to remember the hitch in her breathing when his hands trailed up her middle to find her twin mounds. And she would never forget the instant reaction of her nipples when they hardened at his touch. Passion bit her, causing her to moan from the exquisite heat making her brazen and insistent.

One of her legs hooked around him and she pressed herself into what she could feel was a rigid erection. Before, when passion overtook them, she'd experienced some of the same flames rocketing inside of her now, that left her panties damp and an ache at the meeting of her thighs. However, they'd thought it best to not move things to the next level with such an unstable future.

But to hell with all of that, she was twenty-two years old, getting left with a broken heart anyway, so she wanted to love him in every way a woman could love a man.

Standing in front of her door with the light of the microwave flashing forever midnight, time stood still, but his hands roamed—testing her endurance for temptation and treating her to a scalding introduction to intimacy at its most natural form. Her body trembled as his fingers searched for the ultimate beacon. She was a lighthouse bringing her man in from waves that were threatening to drown them both.

When his fingers found the slit into her soul, a hiss slid through her teeth and she knew she wouldn't be able to remain on her feet long. He must've known as well, because he lifted her and carried her into the room he'd never seen before and placed her on the bed where the bedside lamp bathed them in a soft glow. She looked up at him and he looked *into* her. She felt exposed and it was alright, because it was Terry. It was the most intimate moment of the evening.

Symphony sat up when he didn't seem to want to move his eyes away from her. She reached for his belt, undid the buckle and button on his pants, and slowly unzipped them. He unbuttoned the shirt and tossed it somewhere in the room. She looked up at him and saw him watching her. Their eyes held as she slowly pulled down his slacks and boxers. She felt him come free from the boxers before she saw him. She had never seen a naked man before, but to her eyes, he was perfect. Perfectly made. She pushed the unwelcomed thought that he was not perfectly made for her, aside for now.

Tonight he would be.

Looking back up at him she tentatively placed a hand over his erection and his eyes slid shut. The skin was velvety soft and hard at the same time. It sent a thrill of excitement through her. She stroked it, experimenting with the feel of him.

What a novelty.

Terry placed a gentle hand on hers and quietly pushed her back onto the bed. She was nervous, excited, and lost in the enormity of it all.

Her panties sliding down her thighs were sending currents of electricity through her, making her skin sensitive and expectant. Next, her nightgown was removed and tossed into the darkness where caution and restraint lie.

She'd told him once that she was on the pill to regulate her periods, so when he lifted a questioning brow as he waited firmly at her slick entrance, she gave a brief shake of her head. His eyes closed a moment and he gave her a ghost of a smile.

She felt him ease inside of her—a foreign full feeling. From his hesitation, she could tell he was apprehensive about hurting her. She reached up and pulled him to her. He captured her mouth at the same moment he entered her and swallowed the small cry of the pain.

Oh goodness, she didn't know it would hurt that much. He stilled inside of her and she wasn't sure if she could go on, but then she felt her body adjusting to him as he slowly pulled out and eased back in again. Every time he moved in and out of her, the pain pushed further and further away, until it was gone and pleasure was left in its place. Waves and waves of it were building up as she began to meet him thrust for thrust.

He buried himself deep inside of her, but she couldn't seem to get enough of him. Her back arched and her hips thrust to meet his every plunge. She wished she could box up the pleasure and store it for later.

How could she let him go?

Why couldn't they be on the same road?

A life with Terry flashed across her mind, but she refused to be plagued by "what ifs" and impossibilities.

Sweet tortuous flames licked her from her toes to the lobes of her ears and the notes from a beautiful opus played in her head. The bows slid fiercely across the strings, the flutes soared higher and higher, the rapid keys of a piano danced across her breast, all directed by her maestro, sending the song higher and higher into the rafters until the culmination of notes were too great to hold.

"Terry!"

"Symphony!"

The simultaneous cries came with their release. The only words spoken, because no others were needed, in the wake of their passionate goodbye.

Symphony stared at the wood beams above her wishing she could erase the regret that squeezed itself into every pore of her body. Terry was gone and there was nothing she could do about it. Their time together had been brief, but in that short span, she'd grown to care deeply about him.

She lay there on the floor with flour itching the side of her face, knowing she would get up soon, go to her workstation, and create something just for him.

Chapter 4

Symphony folded herself into her robe on her oversized chair and felt physically and mentally drained from the day. She'd finally pushed Terry from her mind and concentrated on replacing the mixer. It would be a huge dent in her budget, but that's because she was so strict with her spending. Most of the money from the bakery went into a savings account that she never touched, the rest she used to pay herself a modest living and run the business.

She managed her business well and her profits had not shown any declines since she'd re-opened it under her name. On the contrary, her business did so well, that she could retire right now if she was so inclined, and be just fine.

Some of her fatigue also stemmed from Cooper Read. He was the slick-talking corporate representative of a frozen pie and pastry company out of Louisiana, who was trying to convince her to let them market and sell her lemon croissants. He had no idea how to take "no" for an answer. Read wasn't the only one; there were several others like him slithering about. He was just the one who hissed the loudest.

Symphony

Symphony found herself requiring her staff to sign nondisclosure agreements and increasing the security at her store. She was also very careful about her hiring process. She did a thorough background check on all the people she hired, even for the catering side of her business. Not because she was afraid of someone stealing her money, but rather her recipes and combinations of ingredients left in the cooler.

Sipping a huge mug of tea at the end of the day was her evening routine. Even though she would have to be up at four to get to the bakery by five for the morning prep, she never found herself able to go to sleep before eleven. With her eyes closed and her hands warming on the mug, she settled into her chair, letting the day fall off of her. She took a sip and smiled, never tiring of the sweet cinnamon and apples flavoring her tea.

Her eyes flew open at the sound of her ringing cell phone. Symphony looked across the room at the large wall clock in the kitchen.

10:57

Who in the world would be calling her at this hour? Very few people had her cell phone number. Her aunt of course and Ian in case of emergencies. There were a handful of others, but that's it.

Symphony

Thinking that if Cooper Read had gotten hold of her cell number, she would castrate him for using it and for calling so late. She placed the mug on the side table and ran to the kitchen to her purse where she'd left it on one of the bar stools around her island.

By the time she retrieved it from her purse, she'd missed the call. There was no name and the number was unfamiliar, though it was from her aunt's area code. Before she could call it back, the phone rang again.

"Hello?" Symphony's voice was uncertain and curious.

"Hi, Dear. Is this Symphony?" Asked an unfamiliar female voice. "I'm terribly sorry for calling at this hour."

"Yes, who is this?" She asked, a little harsher than she intended to sound. Fear gripped her throat as she braced herself for bad news—which always came unexpectedly and at unorthodox hours, such as this.

"This is your aunt Helen's friend, Gloria. She asked me to call you if she made a turn for the worse."

Symphony's hand clutched her throat, willing it not to suffocate her. "The worse? What're you talking about? Is Aunt Helen ill?" She managed to say.

"I'm sorry, Symphony, I thought you were aware of her condition."

47

Symphony

"Condition?"

"Yes. I…uh…" There was a long pause. "Helen assured me that she'd spoken to you." Another pause.

"Spoken to me about what? What are you trying to tell me? What's the matter with Aunt Helen?"

The questions tumbled out of her. Upon saying her aunt's name, the overwhelming grief of the day consumed her and her aunt's name was accompanied with a sob. She folded into a heap on her kitchen floor too afraid to face a reality that was likely to break her.

Helen Cole was Symphony's world. She'd raised her when her parents refused to. Her aunt Helen was her only constant in her life while growing up and she wasn't sure she could face a world that didn't have her in it.

She could still remember the dress she'd worn when her momma had gotten her ready for church that day—*the* day. It was too short for her four-year old self, but still the best one she had and one of her favorite things to wear. She loved the yellow daisies on the sky-blue dress and how the blue made the flowers look as if they were blowing in the breeze when she moved. Her socks were too thick for the black patent leather shoes she wore and made her feet hurt with each step, but Symphony knew that complaining would only get her popped across the thigh, so she pretended they were fine.

She didn't care anyway, because she was going to church with Aunt Helen and afterwards there would be lunch and the best desserts—the only desserts she every got. Sometimes, the only days she ever got a full meal. There were never any treats at her house.

For some reason her momma had been especially nice to her that day. She'd never taken the time to part and brush her thick mass of hair so carefully unless it was a special occasion. Usually the special occasion had something to do with Ms. Franklin, the white lady who smelled nice and always carried a bunch of papers in her hands. On those days, she remembered her momma taking the time to clean the house and making sure she was dressed nice and clean as well.

"Get your pink suitcase." Her momma said, harshly.

"Am I spending the night?" Symphony asked, almost too afraid to hope that she would be away from her parents for any length of time. Well, they weren't actually ever around. She was just always left with the neighbor or some kid who wasn't too much older than she was. But she never got to stay all night with Aunt Helen. She had a feeling that it was simply because her momma knew it would make her happy and she did everything she could to keep her miserable.

"Just get the damn suitcase!" She snapped. "Can't you ever do anything without asking a million questions?"

Symphony didn't say anything else, but she dared hoped that by some miracle, Aunt Helen would never let her go once she got to her house.

And she didn't.

Symphony later found out that the lady who would visit every so often was a social worker who was assigned to do home checks, because her parents were getting government assistance. She also hadn't known that her aunt had been trying to fight her baby sister for custody since Symphony was born.

It took four years but she'd won on the grounds that her parents were on drugs and unfit to care for their child. It also took them getting involved in a drug and human trafficking ring for the state to finally remove Symphony from the home.

Symphony never looked back.

"Hello? Hello?" She heard the woman say, bringing her back to a reality she wanted no part of.

"Tell me." She said finally, just barely audible. "What's wrong with her?"

Symphony

"She has cancer and we fear that she won't be with us long. You better get here quickly."

Chapter 5

Symphony's flight was at 6am, so she was up all night preparing her bakery stock for her departure. She wasn't sure how long she would be gone, but she was planning for several days. Ian was more than capable of handling the bakery in her absence. The only thing he couldn't do was introduce a new original recipe of the week.

Or could he?

Should she let him spread his wings?

Just in case, she left him with two weeks' worth of previously used specialty recipes, from a few years ago—some that she hadn't turned into regular bakery menu items.

Symphony stood in the middle of her kitchen. The music danced with the delicious notes spilling from the ovens. Prep took longer than normal, because she had to use the smaller mixer—the new one wouldn't arrive for another two days. Instead of thinking about the traitorous appliance, she directed all of her focus on preparing her bakery for her absence. She just prayed Marylyn and Stephanie showed up on time, every day.

Symphony

Ian arrived just after 3am, surprised to see her there, totally absorbed in the music and baking. He didn't ask any questions; he just jumped right in and began straightening the work stations and panning dough. After everything was prepped and put away, he turned a questioning eye to her. She asked him to step into the office with her.

Symphony knew she didn't have to worry about Ian and Ricco. They'd been with her for years. Ian stood stoically in the doorway with his hands behind his back, waiting expectantly. He looked like an Ian. Tall, pale, English-like, and very serious like most Englishmen, with the exception of the dialect. Ian was from Hawaii, of all places—born and raised.

When she explained to him that she would be gone for at least a week, besides the initial widening of his eyes, he embraced the enormity of the responsibility she was handing him with quiet professionalism. She decided at that moment to completely hand over the reins.

"Feel free to flex your creative muscles, if you like and serve creations of your own. Change the name on the chalkboard from 'Symphony's Original' to 'Ian's Original.'"

Symphony

His stone-face gave nothing away, yet the throbbing near his temple belied his excitement for the opportunity she was giving him.

"No one is allowed in our kitchen, except you and Ricco. Without exception." He nodded his understanding. "Tell Ricco, she needs to come in earlier, while I'm gone." Symphony knew the tiny, vivacious Naricco Maki would have no problem. She was always asking for more responsibility, but Symphony being the control freak that she knew she was, always felt the need to be involved in most aspects of the kitchen, leaving only the menial jobs for Ricco.

Symphony suddenly realized how selfish she'd become in her bakery. Leaving Ian and Ricco in control of it now, felt like what she assumed a mom would feel when leaving her baby for the first time.

Would she ever be a mom?

No.

For that, she would need a husband, and unless... She couldn't let her thoughts go there, not now. Not today.

"Yes, ma'am." Ian turned to walk back into the kitchen, she knew, to make sure Ricco was starting on the pre-orders for the day. He turned back to her. "What about when they bring the new mixer?"

Symphony

"They are to deliver it where all deliveries go."

She had an entrance, not so unlike a mud room, between the entrance of the building and the entrance of her kitchen for the purpose of deliveries. She'd had to add it when other bakeries were sending "spies" to find out some of her pastry secrets, disguised as delivery people. Plus, it kept dirt and germs from her work areas.

"Yes, ma'am." He replied again. "We'll get it hooked up."

"If you need help with getting the mixer in place, let me know and I'll get someone to help you." He nodded, again. "Then Symphony's is yours until I return."

"Oh, no ma'am, I couldn't possibly be so presumptuous to ever think of Symphony's as mine, but I will take care of it just as you do, to the best of my ability."

She nodded firmly, appreciating his loyalty.

"I hope your aunt Helen pulls through." He offered sincerely and in an unprecedented show of emotion, Symphony's eyes spilled with the tears she'd held since the call from the lady named Gloria.

Ian was sensitive enough not to react to the tears. Instead, he said, "I will take care of everything, just as if you were here."

Symphony

She smiled and watched him walk into the kitchen. She knew he would do as he said and she would try not to worry.

Apparently, everyone in the city of Jacksonville was flying out of town before the crack of dawn, today. It was the closest airport she could get to from St. Augustine. The TSA line snaked around in an infuriating coil. And why do they taunt people with a Starbucks right next to security when it's against rules and regulations to bring it through the blasted security check point, she thought. There better be one on the other side, she continued to muse. She had a box of pastries for herself and Aunt Helen and she wanted coffee to go with one while she waited for her flight.

"Irony is feeling violated going through security." Symphony instinctively turned to the deep invasive sound of a man speaking behind her that was much too close to her ear. So close, she could feel the vibrations of his voice as the sound traveled to her brain. She turned, sour-faced and decidedly irritated towards the intrusion of her personal space and met vibrant expectant blue eyes.

Why was he talking to her? What was she supposed to say to that? However, she couldn't wonder long.

Symphony

"Next!" The TSA security officer shouted into the crowd. Symphony quickly dismissed the guy and gave the necessary information to the agent before she was ushered into yet another line for the *violation*, as the stranger so aptly pronounced.

She placed her shoes and briefcase in one bin and her small purse and box of pastries in another. She couldn't help but think of the man's comments as she was asked to stand on the outline of feet and lift her arms as the machine pierced its x-ray vision eyes through her. She grabbed up her things from the bins and strode briskly away to put on her shoes.

Walking to her gate, Symphony watched a woman struggling with directing her three small kids to their gate. Each kid had a backpack that was almost as big as they were. Even the one in the stroller had a bag hanging on to it. The little one in the stroller dropped what looked like a tiny stuffed cat. Symphony picked it up.

"Ma'am!" There was so much noise from the passenger-choked terminal and constant announcements. "Ma'am!" She called out again.

The woman stopped at the urging of her son who was nearly running to keep up with her. She smiled appreciatively when she spotted the little gray cat in Symphony's outstretched hand.

Symphony

"Kitty!" The little girl in the stroller, screeched. "Gimmie!" Her little chubby hands demanded her toy.

"What do you say, Emily?"

"Tank youuu." The little girl sang out. The mom mouthed the words "Thank You," before steering her small entourage away. The little girl, Emily, peered over the side, smiled, and waved at Symphony until it was too difficult for her to do so. "Come on. We need to get seated on the plane so we won't be late getting back to Daddy." She heard the woman say to the kids.

Symphony wondered briefly again if there would ever be little faces that were similar to her own.

She adjusted the strap of her leather satchel and spotted the Starbucks at last. Of course she was very partial to her own coffee she sold in her shop, but didn't dwell on it since it wasn't an option.

Seated at the gate with the steaming coffee and pastry in hand she closed her eyes as her teeth sank into the flaky lemon and honey croissant. She didn't often indulge in her pastries, but she needed the sugar today. Her emotions were all over the place and since she couldn't be in her kitchen baking, she needed to at least indulge in a scrumptious treat.

"I love that place." The voice stated enthusiastically, ruining her tiny moment of peace.

Her lids eased open, turning to glare at the intruder, which turned out to be the same as from the TSA line.

"What?" She asked in an exasperated voice, determined to warn him off.

"Symphony's," he motioned towards the pastel green box in her lap. "I love that place."

Clearly, her abrasive tone had not offended him like she'd hoped. She gave him a tight smile and dragged her eyes away from his dancing blue ones. Symphony turned her body slightly away from him, leaving no doubt that she didn't want to be bothered.

"Are you bringing those to someone or do you love them as much as I do to buy a box at a time?"

Symphony huffed and rolled her eyes to the ceiling.

What the hell? Why is this beach bum talking to me?

She turned to look at him fully and slowly lugged her eyes from his worn black flip-flops, up his tanned legs not missing the worn khaki cargo shorts to his Loony Toons t-shirt with a graphic of Bugs Bunny on it. Framed by his sun-bleached hair that fell just passed his ears, she finally rested her eyes on his equally tanned face.

Symphony

He'd watched her leisurely perusal of him and when her gaze met his, he gave her an appreciative, flirtatious smile. Symphony was ill prepared, beach bum or not, he was sexy as sin and ruggedly handsome. The flippant retort on her tongue, dissolved and instead she felt confusion as she didn't know how to respond. Relieved that she didn't have to, the airline representative announced the boarding of first class passengers.

She'd decided to upgrade her ticket when she noticed the large crowd waiting at the gate. "Excuse me, I need to board." She tossed over her shoulder as she picked up her satchel and purse and hoped she would get to enjoy her coffee on the plane.

Storing her satchel in the overhead bin, Symphony settled into her window seat, wanting the spot next to her to remain empty. She placed the box on the floor at her feet and fished her phone from her purse to send Gloria, Aunt Helen's friend, a text to let her know she was on her way. She put the phone away and stared out of the window after pulling the half eaten pastry from the box. She took a bite, not giving a damn that the tissue paper seemed to crinkle much too loudly, and she sipped her coffee.

Sighing heavily, she watched the men outside roll away on the luggage carrier. Then she was staring at nothing at all when she saw her future clearly through the dark. It was professionally successful, bleak, and lonely. She felt hollow and instantly wanted to be filled with something, but didn't know what.

Feeling someone sit next to her, she inwardly groaned. Keeping her eyes on the window, she heard the click of the seatbelt. She just hoped like hell that whomever it was didn't want to talk…at all.

The safety measures and pre-flight checks fell into a hush in the background. The lights around the airport blinked in the darkness of the pre-dawn as she slid down the window cover, closed her eyes, and clutched the cup in her hand.

The plane backed away from the gate and rolled off onto the runway. "Good morning folks, we've been given clearance for takeoff…" The pilot droned on, but Symphony wasn't paying attention. It didn't take long for her to feel the plane pick up speed and lift. She was leaving Jacksonville. It had been years since she'd left Florida—too busy building her business. Symphony brought the coffee to her lips again and tried to let the warm sweet liquid heat the icy edges of fear that pricked her. She was worried about her aunt.

Symphony

"Have you ever seen the sun rise while you're above the clouds?" She instinctively knew who the male voice next to her belonged to.

"What?" She opened her eyes, annoyed, and turned to the culprit, feeling she would never get to enjoy her coffee. Just as she thought, it was the talkative guy from the airport.

"The sunrise? Have you ever viewed it from above the clouds?" He leaned over and lifted the visor that covered the window.

Shocked by his audacity to reach over her, she just stared at him. With his chin, he directed her to look out. Reluctantly, she turned to the window. Through the small opening, she could see the sky waking up. The sun kissed the heavens and blazed streaks of burnt orange, yellow, and dare she say, sky blue, for as far as she could see. The clouds were a pillow of cotton balls. Then she saw a patch that seemed to take on shapes. She leaned closer to the window.

From her perspective it looked like they were floating over a field of bunnies. It was incredible. She'd never seen anything like it.

He leaned across her.

Pulling her pastry and coffee to her chest, she was at a loss. He was leaning across her like they were traveling buddies.

They were not traveling buddies!

So why did he feel comfortable enough to violate her boundaries.

"Do you see the elephant?" He asked her, ignoring her bewildered expression.

She wanted so badly to look out to see what he was talking about, but sat stonily in the seat instead, clutching her breakfast as if a tiger was at her feet.

He looked at her expectantly and when she looked back as if he was a lunatic, his lips twitched with amusement. She had a feeling the he was privately mocking her.

Continuing to ignore her lethal stares he said, "Those clouds look like they're saying, 'Hey!'" He called out the last word as if he was talking across the aisle. Self-consciously, she looked around to see if people were staring at them. She could only get a tiny glimpse of the people directly across the aisle and they didn't seem to be paying any attention.

How could he be so animated? Surely he was not getting the warm and fuzzies from her, so why wouldn't he just shut up and leave her alone?

Symphony

And he was leaning into her private space for far too long—so close to her that the subtle scent he wore gently tugged her unconsciously toward him. Damn he smelled good. That pissed her off too.

When there were only the sweet scents of the bakery threading through her every pore, day in and day out, it made her even more sensitive to his masculine fragrance—a blend of clean woods, citrus, and the ocean breeze.

She said nothing. Turning to look at her, he finally resigned to easing back into his space. "But, can you blame them? I've been wanting to say it since I saw you in the boarding line."

Her eyes followed him back to his side of their seats and she gave him a tight-lipped shadow of a smile—her only response to his comment. However, grateful he'd moved away, his absence caused her to close her eyes concentrating on the fading trails of his scent before deciding what in the world she would do about him for the rest of the flight. He obviously wasn't going to leave her alone until she offered him some form of conversation. He adjusted in his seat allowing a soft ribbon of his scent to play with her senses again.

She appreciated a man who didn't drown himself in a fragrance. A woman would have to be intimately close to this man to know he was even wearing it and she could just imagine someone snuggled up to him being seduced by it and him.

Symphony took a deep breath and sent it out in a rush. Sipping at her coffee she found it too cool to drink; she especially liked it piping hot; this cup was twenty minutes too late for that.

Wanting to glare at him for keeping her away from her caffeine fix, she decided it just wasn't worth the hassle. Miraculously, though, he didn't say another word.

Because she hadn't slept all night, it didn't take long for her to drift soundlessly into darkness.

When she woke, she noticed her tray was down and the coffee and pastry was sitting atop it. Had she put them there? Doubting seriously that she had and knowing her *dawn* expert was most likely responsible for the kindness, she wasn't quite ready to look his way. Who was this guy who had her talking about bunnies and seeing elephants in the clouds?

When she looked out of the window again, it was a haze blue, nondescript and unremarkable.

"So what does a guy have to do to get into your box?"

She turned from the window, "Excuse me?"

His blue eyes widened in alarm. "I'm sorry," he chuckled, "that came out so wrong."

She couldn't help but smile and push the thought of him getting into her "box" to the back of her mind. Symphony found that she couldn't resist this man who was probably just a nice guy—what woman could? She knew she was probably especially bitchy these days because it had been so long since she had a distraction of the sexual nature. She was at least tolerable when she had been hooking up with Eric.

Symphony held this stranger's eyes for a moment and then caught the attention of a flight attendant. She handed her the Starbucks cup and asked for coffee for them both. She looked at her seat partner and lifted a brow for confirmation.

"Sure, I'll have coffee too." He said, agreeably.

With the tray back in place, she leaned down and awkwardly picked up the box at her feet and placed it into his hands.

"Help yourself," she stated.

"I won't deprive you of more than one," he said, taking the box without hesitation. "I know how sacred Symphony's are." He pulled out a Europe-styled croissant typically with a chocolate line in it, but hers had chocolate along with thinly sliced strawberries and baked apples.

Symphony

She watched him take a generous bite. His tongue slipped out trailing the bite and removing flaky bits of croissant from his lips. That ordinary act tugged at a familiar spot in her core. Her eyes watched him chew something she'd made with her own hands and it was making her dizzy. That first bite seemed to play out in slow motion. She was transfixed.

It took her a moment to notice his mouth was no longer moving. Instead, it was smiling knowingly at her. Her face burned with embarrassment. He handed the box back to her. When she didn't respond, he joked, "I'll be more than happy to keep them. This woman is a genius in the kitchen. If I ever meet her, she may be in jeopardy of a kidnaping."

"Yea?" She asked, amused and a little flattered.

"Absolutely."

"Then what?"

"Locked in the highest tower with an oven and no chance of escape."

"Why would you do that?"

"Because I like sweets, plus I heard she's a bitch anyway. So throwing her in a tower would be good for mankind." He paused and his smile widened. "The best of situations."

"A bitch, huh? Is that so?" She knew that's what most people probably thought of her, because of the things she'd overheard and she knew she wasn't the friendliest person around, but to hear someone actually say it…it made her feel…well, it hurt her feelings.

"Yes." He stated with finality, not noticing the hurt look in her eyes. He popped the last bit of pastry in his mouth. "I've never had that one."

Her mood brightened by his satisfied grin. "It was something she tried on a whim." She told him. "Liked it?" She asked. She had no idea why this guy's approval was so important, but she hoped he thought it was delicious.

Just then the flight attendant returned with their coffee. He was about to say something, but she held up her hand. Symphony picked up her coffee and took a tentative sip. Perfect, she thought. Not nearly as good as hers or Starbucks, but she needed the hot jolt of caffeine. Still holding her hand towards him to stifle any attempt at conversation, she closed her eyes and took a few more sips before she put the cup on the tray and turned slowly to him.

"I've been trying to do that all morning." She directed soft accusing eyes at him. "Now, you were saying?"

His sheepish smile told her he knew what she was hinting at.

"How could I not? Is what I was saying. How could I not love it? Everything she has is delicious, I don't care if people says she's a bitch. Someone who can bake like this can't be all bad." He brushed the crumbs from his hands and held out his right one to her.

"Kyle Dean. Thank you for sharing."

She took his hand in hers. It was warm and strong—like her coffee.

"Symphony James." She smiled as if she'd just revealed a huge secret and she guess she had, in a way. "Do I need security?"

Kyle simply stared at her for at least ten seconds

"You can't be the Symphony of Symphony's." He stuttered.

"And why not?"

"Because that would mean that the sweet taste of pastry I just ate, would be soiled by the foot jammed in my mouth. I'm so sorry if I've offended you."

She gave him a rare grin. "No offense taken. I *can* be a bitch at times, but I'll try to work on that."

He leaned in slightly towards her and whispered, "If you married me, your name would be Symphony James Dean…Pretty bad-ass, huh?"

Chapter 6

Symphony stared out the window, looking down at the patchwork of land below. *Symphony James Dean.* The name circled her mind attached to pink helium-filled balloons and the smell of cinnamon rolls.

As much as people hate to be compared with others, especially in the case of relationships, it's nearly impossible not to compare what you've never had to even the slightest hint of a possibility—real or imaginary.

Terry had never even kidded about the idea. And yet, this man, this stranger, even though she knew he was purely flirting, the fact that he'd formed the words made her envision, if only for a moment, a life with Kyle Dean.

She wondered if his lips would be soft when he kissed her goodbye in the mornings or if he would make coffee while she got ready for work. She wondered if he would be the type of husband who called his wife in the middle of the day just to say "hi" or brought home random gifts on a whim. Symphony wondered if they would become a couple who had to schedule a time for sex, not have it at all, or the type of couple who couldn't get enough of each other.

And then inwardly berated herself for her thoughts.

"So are your parents proud as punch that you are *the* Symphony of Symphony's"

Never had she met a man who'd said, "proud as punch." For some reason the phrase made her think of the sliced oranges that would be waiting on the counter when she got home from school.

She turned to him. "I grew up with my aunt." The words were casual, though she felt anything but, on this subject.

"Oh I'm sorry." He said sincerely. "When did you lose them?"

"Oh, they aren't lost. They just lost the privilege of having a kid, because of drugs and the state kind of frowns upon conducting a human trafficking ring around small children." She had no idea why she'd shared that very private bit of her life with this stranger.

But if the comment shocked him, he didn't let on. He didn't have a flippant retort, offer his condolences, nor did he give her the look her friends' parents had given her when they found out she was Helen Cole's little niece.

Symphony

That poor little girl. Tsk...tsk...tsk.

The look was mixed with pity and awkward silence.

Instead, he looked her straight in the eyes and said, "How long did it take before you were out baking your aunt?"

"Much longer than I'd anticipated." She answered through quiet laughter, trying not to disturb the other passengers. "She's very good." She cocked her head to the side. "How did you know she baked?"

"Just a guess." He said with a shrug. "Tell me a lesson that she taught you growing up."

Symphony held Kyle's blue eyes for a long moment. She looked at him as if she didn't know what to make of him, but couldn't keep herself from this conversation. His questions intrigued her.

"She taught me to always give back. No matter how much or how little you have, there's always a way to help others."

"And do you...help others?"

"I do."

"Personally or through your business?"

"They are one in the same. My business is my life. Baking is what I am, who I am. So I donate all the leftover food to shelters in the area as well as sponsor a Cookies and Milk Night for women and children living at a shelter specifically for victims of domestic abuse in Jacksonville."

"There's other things that you do, don't you? That few people know about?"

"I do what I can."

"Not many people know the real you." It was a statement that he seemed pretty sure of. How could he make such a claim? He was right, of course. Like he'd said already, most people pegged her as a bitch. She didn't consider herself a philanthropist, just a person who knew what it was like not to have anything sweet in her life.

She shrugged her shoulders and he sensed that she didn't like talking about herself.

She wanted the light to spin onto him. "Tell me something you used to love to do as a kid."

"Play cards." He admitted without hesitation. "By the time I was ten, I was cleaning out all my dad's friends at the poker table."

They talked about everything and nothing for the rest of the flight. It was a great distraction from what she may be facing when she got to South Carolina. To her surprise, Kyle pulled out a deck of cards and taught her how to play some card game she'd never heard of. She beat him twice.

Symphony

They finished the rest of the pastries talking about places they'd visited and their favorite animal at the zoo. Both favored the big cats, but found that they didn't care much for their domestic brethren. The flight was over quickly and it was time to say goodbye to Kyle Dean.

The Charleston airport had changed a lot since the last time she'd visited. Had that been nearly six years ago? Symphony was surprised to see a man holding a card with her name on it at baggage claim. Gloria had obviously gotten her text and sent someone to pick her up. How thoughtful.

The oppressive August heat was still the same—stifling and sticky. Symphony watched T.J., the man who was bringing her to Gwenda Island where her aunt lived, and noticed he didn't look at all like any driver she'd imagined. He had her luggage and was a few steps ahead of her, dressed more like Kyle than some of the other drivers waiting on their passengers.

Thinking about Kyle made her glance around to see if she saw him. He'd said that he was visiting the Charleston area on business and a little pleasure, but didn't say what kind, and she didn't ask. That was his business. Though, she was a bit disappointed that they didn't get a chance to say one last goodbye.

Symphony

By all accounts, she had enjoyed talking with him during the flight. Other than the marriage comment, he hadn't made a pass at her or made her feel uncomfortable by pressing her to go out with him, like some men had when she was forced to mingle with the public.

She looked around one last time before she climbed into the black BMW. She wondered briefly if Gloria had used a service or if she owned this car.

The moment the car pulled away, her eyes closed. She remembered the tender squeeze Kyle had given her hand when she told him why she was flying to Charleston. He hadn't said that everything would be alright or that he hoped her aunt pulled through, he'd said, "Cry when you're sad, scream when you're angry, and punch something if you need to. Do not apologize for your feelings; they belong to you and only you."

No one had ever said anything like that to her. It was as if he truly knew her and about her stoic control in which she shielded herself. His words made her feel as if everything, in fact, would be ok.

"Ms. James?" Symphony squinted up at T.J. standing in the car door. "We're here, Ma'am. We need to take the boat the rest of the way."

Symphony

They were at the Charleston Harbor. All manner of marine vessels could be seen. "Are we here already?"

"Yes ma'am. And I had to stop by the deli to pick up something for Ms. Gloria. I didn't have the heart to wake you. The reception is going to be a lovely affair."

"Reception?"

"Yes, aren't you here for her nephew's wedding reception?"

She shook her head no, took his out stretched hand, and eased onto legs that could barely hold the rest of her exhausted self. "Welcome to Charleston, anyway." A look of surprise flashed across his face. "Oh sorry Miss. Are you Ms. Helen's niece?" She nodded feeling the enormity of why she was here.

"Fine lady, Ms. Helen. Fine, fine lady."

Smoothing the gray sundress and removing the yellow jacket she'd worn on the plane, she followed T.J. to the end of the pier where she noticed a few others waiting, probably to go to one of the many islands dotting the coast.

"Now, I really think you may want to be kidnapped." Kyle teased her as she walked towards the *boat* that she assumed was going to take her to Gwenda. It was much larger than the ferry that had brought her to her aunt's part of the island in the past or Aunt Helen's sail boat. She wondered if this too, belonged to Gloria.

Kyle whistled loudly when he saw where she was heading and Symphony was surprised by how glad she was to see him again.

"Everywhere I turn, there you are." He said.

"Everywhere I turn, there *you* are." She threw back at him.

"I'm not complaining." His voiced in and undertone and sincerity lit his face.

She cocked an eye at him. He had a way about him that could make a girl throw caution to the wind and dare him to kidnap her. But not today.

"It was a pleasure meeting you, Mr. Dean."

"Dean? I get so tired of that name. From now on, I'm simply Kyle."

His statement made her wonder why he didn't want to be addressed by his last name. She also wondered what he did for a living, but since he hadn't brought it up, she wouldn't either.

"Ok, Kyle, it was a pleasure meeting you."

"It's a pleasure you can relive over and over."

She looked up into darkening eyes and nearly melted. His confidence was so damned alluring.

Symphony

Symphony could see T.J. waiting patiently for her. "Where're you headed?" She heard herself ask Kyle.

"The charter I'd arranged isn't here yet and I have to meet someone in about thirty minutes." He said, looking out over the water, shielding his eyes from the sun.

"Which island?" She asked, curious about the island and who he had to meet. Was it a woman?

"Kiawah."

"Where the big resort is?"

"Yes, would you happen to be going there too?"

"No, my aunt owns half of a private island near here."

His brows lifted in surprise and he glanced at the yacht.

"*This* isn't hers and the island is simply a small patch of land surrounded by water." She said quickly while pointing at the vessel. "It belongs to a friend of hers." Symphony turned to T.J. "T.J., can we give Mr.—" she caught herself, "Can we give *Kyle* a ride to Kiawah. If I remember correctly, it's not too far out of the way?"

"Yes. No problem."

Symphony

Bubbles of excitement burst inside of her. She enjoyed Kyle's company and refused to feel guilty about experiencing this tiny bit of happiness knowing her aunt was so sick. She knew Aunt Helen well and her aunt would not begrudge her any happiness no matter what.

The desolation she felt just yesterday was a distant memory. Even if she never saw Kyle again, there was a light inside of her now that she didn't want to extinguish. Yesterday she was lying on the floor with her face caked in flour. Today she was sailing up the cost of South Carolina with a handsome stranger named Kyle.

The irony surrounding the circumstances of how they met, was not lost on her.

Chapter 7

Symphony didn't recognize the shrunken form she saw in Aunt Helen's bed. She turned questioning eyes to Gloria who was standing quietly in the doorway of the bedroom.

"She's been holding on to see you, Dear."

Symphony walked over to her and reached for the frail hand that used to knead dough better than any machine and make the best treats with scraps that most people would throw away.

These hands, with their creased skin, brown and paper-thin, had eased the aches from bruises, held her hand when she was nervous, and prayed fervently with her at night and at every mealtime. She held the lithe fingers and let the tears fall. They were heavy drops of misery that tasted like empty corridors twisting endlessly around like a maze.

"Why didn't you tell me?" She whispered through the tightening of her throat.

"Because I'm a seventy-two-year-old grown woman and am allowed to have secrets. Besides, you had your own life to live. There was nothing you could've done." She hadn't expected and answer, but the strength in Aunt Helen's voice had not diminished.

Symphony

"Hello there." Sitting gingerly on the bed next to her, Symphony smiled through her sadness when she saw her aunt's still bright eyes, full of wisdom and a strength that Symphony always tried to imitate.

"I'm so glad you made it, Baby. Your aunt Ruth has been waiting for me."

Symphony gave her a smile softened with sadness. Ruth was her sister who'd passed away several years ago.

"I just wanted to see you one more time, to know that you were alright. Your heart has been so dark lately." Looking directly at Symphony, her aunt's clear gaze was serious. "You can't let the past taint your future, Baby." Symphony started to speak, but Aunt Helen wouldn't let her. "I don't have long my Sym; let me say my peace."

Aunt Helen gave her an easy smile. "I've loved you since the day you were born and you've always been the daughter of my heart." Symphony wiped her face with the back of her hand and sniffed loudly. "My life was complete when I got to see you grow into a fine woman doing what we always loved to do together." Symphony's heart lifted with the memory.

"I lived my life on my own terms and I was happy. People thought I was crazy for buying this island, and maybe I was a little, but I was happy here. I have no regrets and I don't want you to have any either. Life's too short, Symphony, to live in the dark." Her voice became earnest. "Life is too short for regrets. Follow your heart honey; your brain will eventually catch up."

Symphony thought of Terry Phoenix and didn't know if he was a regret or if it just wasn't the right opportunity. Then she thought about her morning with Kyle and smiled.

"There's a light in you that I haven't seen before." Her weak smile was a shadow of what Symphony remembered it being. "Guard it honey. Don't live for me or anyone else; live for you and everything will be alright."

Symphony had so much she wanted to say, but all she could manage was the most important. "I love you so much Aunt Helen; thank you for loving me." The words rushed out in a gush that almost collapsed her.

"There was no great sacrifice in doing that Sym; you were a wonderful child. And don't go harboring any ill feelings towards your folks." She scolded and for an instant, Symphony was ten again. "The best thing they could do was give you to me, because they knew they couldn't do for you like you needed. Let go any animosity you holding on to, because all it'll do is eat you alive."

Symphony squeezed her aunt's hand while the tears flowed unchecked.

"Stop all that crying now. You're going to be worn out and I need you to make some of those fancy tarts I like and serve them to the folks at the service." Symphony's forehead creased and her lips pressed into a thin line, but she nodded.

"Yes, Ma'am."

"Don't be sad for me. Be happy, Baby Girl. Go out there and find you somebody to love. Life is so much better when you have someone to share your hurts and happiness with." *Oh, if only it were that easy.* Her eyelids fluttered and then gently eased open again. "I'm going to rest now."

Helen Elaine Cole closed her eyes and drifted off to meet her sister, Ruth. She left as peaceful as she lived.

Symphony gathered her into her arms and held her lifeless body as she cried and cried, not knowing how she would live in a world without her aunt.

The Thursday following Aunt Helen's passing was bright, sunny, and pleasantly comfortable. The open window provided a soft breeze that caressed Symphony's face. She wasn't sure how many people to expect for the service, but she made plenty of her aunt's favorites, the tarts included. She also had trays of meats, cheeses, and vegetables for sandwiches, along with coffee, tea, and lemonade.

Aunt Helen's home was grand, larger even than some of the plantation homes in the area. The kitchen was fit for the chef she was, so Symphony felt right at home in it. According to Aunt Helen's lawyer, half of Gwenda Island, this home, and a few other properties in Charleston, now belonged to her. She had no idea her aunts had been so wealthy. All of Ruth's assets, which were substantial, had turned over to Helen and upon Helen's death, everything went to Symphony.

Symphony didn't know what to make of it all at the moment; she just wanted to focus on getting through the day.

Of course Aunt Helen had everything planned out already, to keep from causing any stress to Symphony. And she wasn't stressed, just sad. She'd loved her life with Aunt Helen and was happy for the life she'd given her, but it was difficult not to be sad, no matter what Aunt Helen told her to do.

She thought of Kyle often over the past few days and the words he'd offered her on the plane. *"Cry*

Symphony

when you're sad, scream when you're angry, and
punch something if you need to. Do not apologize for
your feelings; they belong to you and only you." So
she had. She'd cried; she'd screamed; and she hadn't
apologized for any of it.

　　For two days, strangers had moved in and out
of Symphony's personal bubble, normally an
uncomfortable intrusion, yet these people had known
her aunt. They had laughed with their friend Helen,
shared whispers, and so many other things. Somehow,
instead of an intrusion, there was comfort, because all
these people had been a part of her aunt.

　　There was one man in particular, Floyd
Jenkins, whom Symphony suspected was Aunt Helen's
lover. The idea of that was incredible. Symphony
thought her aunt was content with being a loner just as
she was. Hadn't that been the reason she moved to an
island? To get away from others? But according to all
the people she'd met, she'd been quite the social
butterfly. On her visits to her aunt after she'd left
Florida, they had spent time shopping, baking, and just
enjoying the tranquility of being near the water. Why
hadn't she met these people before?

　　Symphony had no answers to her questions, but
she was almost certain that Floyd Jenkins was
someone very special to her aunt. Sadness walked with

him and acute grief coated his features. He seemed to look at everything in the house as if it held a special memory.

Was he the person who'd shared her aunt's hurts and happiness?

Symphony liked Mr. Jenkins. His voice was strong and comforting. The richness of the sound made her think of gourmet hot chocolate. There was a kind of cadence to it that wrapped her in warmth with every word he said.

He'd been over the evening before, while Symphony was busy preparing the food for the luncheon to follow the service and she couldn't find the cream of tartar. "Look behind the coffee in the pantry, Baby." She raised an eyebrow at him and his lips twitched a bit, but he'd picked up his cup of coffee and drank a swallow like they were casually talking about the weather. They hadn't spoken much, but somehow she enjoyed having him there with her in the kitchen—his presence was comforting. She'd wondered if he'd taken that seat time and time before, while watching Aunt Helen move around the kitchen the same way.

Symphony took a deep breath, pushing all thoughts away, so she could focus on what she was doing.

Symphony

The service would start in about fifteen minutes so she decided she'd better head to the pier. She looked out the window at the people gathered at the edge of the water. There were several nice boats bobbing almost in sync.

Symphony placed a hand over her heart, breathed in deeply again, trying to steady the beating against her palm. She walked to the piano where her aunt's urn sat center stage of the living room, and couldn't help sliding onto the bench. Her fingers danced lightly on the keys and the music quieted the voices in her head, screaming at her that, yes, it was perfectly ok to lose her mind.

Looking at the urn atop the piano, she could hear her aunt say, "Play that one I like, Sym."

So she did.

She played a concerto that she'd made up one day when her aunt couldn't get the cd player to start. The song slid from her fingers and when she was done, her spirit felt lighter than it had since receiving the phone call Monday night.

Symphony got up, picked up her aunt's ashes and carried them to the pier where the wind would carry her into the waters that she loved so much.

Everyone was standing underneath the covered area of the pier where she'd often seen her aunt sit and read, but she recently found out that it's where her aunt held parties and danced the night away. Why hadn't she known that side of her mother's sister? Symphony realized that her aunt really did have a full life. She had the life Symphony wanted for herself.

The crowd stood in a semi-circle. In the front, off to the side, Symphony could see most of the people in attendance. Several people spoke during the service. They all had such wonderful things to say. Mr. Jenkins, she noticed, did not speak. He stood like a statue, stoic and unmoving as if trying to keep the cracks from turning him into dust. His demeanor further confirmed to her of his involvement with her aunt. Symphony knew that if she was asked to say anything, the pain would not allow the release of words locked in her throat.

Symphony also noticed Gloria and her husband Dixon. She'd met Gloria's husband Tuesday evening when he came over to meet her and offer his condolences. During the service the pair stood near the preacher as gray as everyone else. Her aunt was loved by everyone she'd met.

She also spotted a few other people she'd met over the past few days. She observed every face, noted every expression. They were solemn, yet there was a crackle of joy she felt from them. These people were proud and pleased to have known Helen Cole. Many of the faces glanced at her from time to time and bestowed kind smiles on here.

Her eyes constantly roamed, because she didn't know where to look, what to do…until…she saw him. She saw him standing there amongst the other mourners and couldn't stop the sunshine that sprang onto her face.

How in the world did Kyle find her?

"Ms. Symphony?" It was Reverend Slate. She turned to him.

"Yes?"

"It's time."

Symphony looked down at the urn cradled in her arm and then back over at Kyle. Somehow she had a feeling that Aunt Helen was up to something.

She walked over to the edge of the pier and before leaning over the railing she pushed a remote for the speaker in the corner and Bach broke through the silence. She could not forget her aunt's love for classical music. Symphony held the urn by its handle and just as she removed the top, a gust of wind blew the contents into the air and Aunt Helen danced with Bach on her grand exit.

Tears pooled in her eyes as she watched her ashes float off. Minutes passed as she looked out over the water, but saw nothing in front of her. And then, she saw her four-year old hands in her aunt's as they danced around the house. She saw the pink plastic bucket she'd surprised her with at the beach one day. They'd made the most beautiful sand castle and moat. She saw the tears her Aunt Helen shed when they had dinner after her graduation, because she was so proud of her. Symphony saw her aunt's smile, her kindness, her love...

She saw her life.

Wonderful. Full. Happy.

"Ms. Symphony." It was Rev. Slate again. She turned shining eyes to him and accepted the comforting pat and gentle grip he gave her shoulder. The reverend took the urn from her. "I'll take this now so you can see to your guests."

One by one, each offered their condolences and spoke of the beautiful service. She invited them to the house for refreshments and her aunt's final request to end the service with the tarts. She shook so many hands and hugged people she'd never laid eyes on.

And then he was there.

An oasis in the middle of the desert.

No longer the beach bum she'd met in the airport. Today, he was dazzlingly handsome in a dark tailored suit, crisp white shirt, and a beautiful lavender and white checked tie, that she had to keep herself from reaching out to touch.

He was breathtaking.

He was here.

"I'm so sorry for your loss." He said, clutching her hand.

Stunned that he was even standing there, she didn't know what to say. He seemed to be drinking her in, just as she was doing to him.

"Have you come to kidnap me?" Her voice quietly serious.

He grinned. "If you like?"

"I would." The words popped out of her mouth on their own—she did not regret them.

His blue eyes held her brown ones, seemingly searching for something.

"Ok." His statement, sure and just as earnest as hers.

She beamed at this man that she hardly knew. "May I ask a favor?" Her words on the edge of a tremble.

"Anything."

"Will you allow me a few moments of sadness and hold me through it." She had no idea why she'd asked such a thing, but knew she needed it, and somehow knew he would give her what she needed.

Symphony

Without saying a word, he opened his arms and she walked into them. Kyle pulled her into the circle of his arms and held her like he'd been doing it all of his life—like he knew exactly what she needed. And for those few moments she grieved for her loss and let herself be held by this stranger. Her soft cries turned into silent shudders of sorrow, but he said nothing. He simply gave her want she wanted.

He held her tightly as if he was trying to absorb her pain. Her soul cried while she keened softly and still, he held her. Kyle said nothing when she quieted and the silence consumed them both. All that could be heard was the gentle lapping of the water hitting the pillars of the pier.

With her eyes closed, she inhaled the soft scent that had seduced her on the airplane and tried to regain her composure. She was not embarrassed or sorry. He had come for this reason; she was sure of it.

When Symphony's anguish had abated, with her face still pressed into his shoulder, her muffled words broke the quiet.

"Thank you." She slowly tried to push away, but he held her a moment longer before opening the space between them. "You smell good." She said.

He chuckled. "You feel good in my arms." He didn't lie.

"Thank you for being here." She whispered, looking up at him. "How'd you know?"

"T.J." His finger twirled a curl framing her face. The intimacy was surprising, though fitting. They looked like two lovers, one comforting the other.

"T.J.?"

"Yea, I saw him at the marina in Charleston."

"Oh?"

She took a deep breath and wiped one of her eyes. Before she could wipe the moisture from the other, he kissed her tears there.

"Let me kiss your tears away." His voice low and inviting.

Not since Terry, had anyone treated her so tenderly. She pushed that thought aside. She didn't want the memory of Terry Phoenix to mar this moment with Kyle.

He took the liberty to sweetly kiss the trail her tears had made, her eyelids, the corners of her mouth. "You're really going to make me kidnap you." He husked out.

"I've given you my permission," she said on a half moan that was surely inappropriate.

Kyle firmly held her head between his hands and placed a soft kiss on her lips. He singed her lips with the tip of his tongue, but held back from greedily mating with her mouth like his life depended on it for nourishment. She could imagine him deepening the kiss and carrying her away from anything that would cause her hurt or pain. With no idea why she was feeling so strongly about this near stranger who could fill her with light in the mist of darkness, he pulled away. They both knew this was not the place nor the time.

"Damn." He breathed, pressing his forehead into hers. "You taste *so* sweet."

"Is that a pun?" She asked smiling up. Her eyes were red and puffy, but she no longer wore the acute sadness she'd felt before. "Come on." She slipped her hand in his and led him to the house. "I have some fabulous pastries I think you may just lose your mind over."

"Well go ahead and book me a room in the insane asylum, now."

Their soft laughter traveled up the path to the house. Many of the guests turned and smiled at them while they mingled among hushed conversations on the patio with plates of the food she'd set out.

She looked over to where Gloria and her husband were standing, heading to thank them for all they'd done. She smiled appreciatively at Gloria. The woman had been a Godsend over the past few days and she could see why her aunt had befriended her. She was meticulous, efficient, and shrewd, but in a nice way. Symphony had also found out that Gloria and her husband, Dixon owned the other half of the island and she couldn't be happier to know her neighbors were these kind people.

Gloria and Dixon were talking to a man she hadn't seen at the service. His back was to her, but she could tell he was about her age, as most of the people at the service had been much older. Something about him was vaguely familiar. Gloria pointed toward her and then frowned slightly when she noticed Symphony was holding Kyle's hand. Symphony wondered what that look was all about. Maybe Gloria was one of those women who had hopes of setting her up with their male kin. Symphony looked over at the guy just as he turned to watch her and Kyle walk up to the patio.

She couldn't breathe.

Terry Phoenix.

What in the hell was he doing here?

Chapter 8

His eyes left her paralyzed. Time whirled. Surprise, confusion, insanity—crisp and clear, clouded her mind. Words fled, leaving her mouth dry and useless. Symphony's ears buzzed as she took in the raw empty echoes of pain Terry's eyes held.

Why?

Terry.

The words from his last letter, those many years ago, came rushing back *"One day, when you're ready to admit you love me, I'm going to walk back into your life and let you."*

Terry Phoenix was back.

Was it just a few days ago, she was thinking about him? *When had she not thought about him?* It was the day she found out about Aunt Helen that she wondered if she'd ever be ready to love; the day before she met Kyle.

Kyle.

She'd finally, finally felt the hope of being lifted from the darkness that had weighed her down for so long. The sadness. The loneness—the guilt, after she'd broken things off with Terry—after they'd gone on their separate paths. Not because she'd met Kyle. It was because she finally realized she could.

Symphony looked up into the uneasy blue eyes of the man standing beside her and then back into Terry's apprehensive ones. The buzzing turned into a roar before darkness claimed her. The kaleidoscope of emotions was too great. Her body was suddenly weak and her legs gave way.

Kyle had noticed the stunned expression on Symphony's face and followed her gaze to the man standing with an older couple he'd seen on the pier. He immediately knew the man was someone from her past. Tension hung thick between Symphony and this guy. She was radiating from it. And then he heard a tiny gasp before she slumped beside him.

"Symphony!" both men exclaimed at once. They took a millisecond to take measure of each other. Kyle pulled Symphony possessively into his arms, his features seized by panic. He had no idea what was going on, although he figured she was extremely overwhelmed.

In the background he heard someone say, "Call the doc."

Kyle caught her and scooped her into his arms with an intimacy he'd never felt before. He knew very little about the woman he held to his chest as he carried her into the house and had no desire to be caught in the middle of anything going on between her and that man who clearly has feelings for her, if the guy's reaction to her fainting was any indication.

He wanted to tell himself that this was not his problem, that Symphony James had no place in his life right now. He didn't have time for whatever any of this was. He should put her down, make sure she was ok, head back to his beach house, and disappear for a while like he'd planned.

However, Kyle couldn't dismiss the fact that it was he who had comforted Symphony moments ago, from grief she couldn't bear on her own. The revelation that she'd chosen to share it with him had touched Kyle greatly. Whatever was going on, he had no time to think about it now.

Symphony knew she was lying down somewhere. Her head hurt like hell and she prayed she was dead, because if what she thought happened had actually happened, she would just die of embarrassment anyway. She knew she must've fainted, so she just tried to hold as still as possible and hope the pain would fade quickly. Relaxing into the cushion, she remembered the last time she'd become so overwhelmed that she'd passed out.

Her mom had shown up at Aunt Helen's, demanding her back. She was high or drunk, it didn't matter which. What mattered was that her mom was behaving like a lunatic—screaming obscenities that sounded foreign in this perfect world that now belonged to her.

There were no roaches taking over the pantry, no stench of spoiled meat festering on the stove, there were no days of hunger so fierce that her stomach screamed in protest, and there were definitely no drunk women, crazy from their last fix.

Not here.

Not in the place that had been a place of happiness, safety, and where home smelled like gingerbread and sugar cookies.

She would die before she was made to leave it.

She'd been so afraid that she would be taken away from a life that she loved, that she'd fainted from the panic and fear. Afterwards, when Aunt Helen gently shook her awake, she remembered feeling just like she did now—like a bull had used her head for a soccer ball.

Immediately, she remembered what caused her to become so overwhelmed. "Terry!" The word ripped from her lips and she instinctively pushed herself up.

Bad move.

Nausea roared, curling her into a fetal position. She stiffened.

"Easy now, Symphony." She heard Gloria's voice gently command.

Symphony trembled, afraid to open her eyes, but knew she had to. Her life had just been kicked in the gut and she could feel the shoe lodged in her head.

"What happened?" The words scratching her throat on their upward climb. Her eyes were still screwed shut, but she was conscious.

"You fainted." Gloria answered her. "Doc thinks it's just the stress of the funeral and everything." Symphony felt a soft hand on her forehead. "Is there anything else that could've caused you to pass out?"

"Doc?" What doctor still made house calls, she wondered.

"Yes, he's a friend in the area. He was already on his way here. He'd been running late because of an accident in town…Now, is there anything else that could've caused you to pass out?"

"No." Her lids lay like weights on her eyes.

Symphony

"Have you eaten, Sweetheart?" She asked, gently.

"Been busy...haven't been hungry." The fog was starting to clear along with the nausea, but the headache was making itself at home. Her voice was weak and raspy.

"You need to take care of yourself."

Symphony struggled to push her lids up. She looked around a moment trying not to move the rest of her and they eased shut again. She was in Aunt Helen's reading den on the sectional sofa.

"It's ok to rest, Symphony. Everyone has been kind enough to pay their respects and leave the island, giving you time to relax."

Symphony was thankful for that. All she wanted to do was sleep. Wait! "What about—"

She opened her eyes to look at Gloria and tried to sit, but gave up the effort quickly.

Gloria stayed her with a pat on her shoulder. "Lie still for a while longer. Kyle and my husband's nephew are waiting to make sure you're ok."

Symphony's brows bunched in confusion, "Your husband's nephew?"

"Terry, is my husband's nephew."

"So, it *was* him that I saw standing with the two of you? How's that possible?"

"We were quite surprised when he told us he knew you and that you were the woman he was heading to Florida to find."

"What?" Her heart constricted. It was a struggle, but she pulled herself up. "To find?" She hadn't been lost. "How did he know I was *here*?"

"It's all quite a coincidence. He came to Gwenda, because we're celebrating the marriage of one of his cousins who recently got married."

Symphony stared at Gloria, she realized the woman had never mentioned her last name. All she knew was Gloria. When she'd first talked to her and found out she was Aunt Helen's friend, she was looking for someone who was elderly—someone who sewed quilts as a hobby and baked cookies for the church. This woman sitting before her, was young enough to still wear heels most fashion models would scratch eyes out for, but old enough to display a kind understanding in her gaze for youthful fools like herself. Not old, but rather she would say, mature, because nothing about Gloria said "old." She was stunning and Symphony could tell Dixon loved his wife. She'd found out yesterday, that the two were only recently married.

"Is Kyle—"

Gloria finished for her. "Yes, he's still here. Both men were quite adamant not to leave until they've seen you."

The other day when Symphony was frustrated with Cooper Read and his pressures of getting her to sell her pastries to a frozen food conglomerate, she thought her well controlled world was complicated enough, but now realized that compared to the death of her aunt, inheriting an island, meeting Kyle Dean, a man who filled her with the whimsy of rainbows, and having Terry Phoenix show up out of nowhere, Cooper Read was just a pebble at the base of a mountain.

"So, what do you want to do?" The green-eyed beauty asked Symphony.

"I want my life back."

Gloria smiled, "This is your life, my dear. Enjoy every single moment of it."

Symphony sighed as she watched Gloria stand, smooth her black skirt, and look at her expectantly.

"I don't have the strength for Terry right now." She slowly closed her eyes and inhaled a deep breath. She was starting to feel normal again, physically, with the exception of the headache. "Tell him whatever you want, but I can't speak to him right now." Her senses could only take so much in one day and her heart had suffered enough with the loss of her aunt. She could not relive a life with Terry right now and wondered if she ever would. She was ready to move forward and wasn't sure if she could with Terry hanging at the edges of her life.

She didn't really want to see anyone, but figured she owed Kyle some sort of explanation.

"I would like to talk to Kyle, if you don't mind."

"Why would I mind?" She gave her a tender knowing smile. "I'll get him." She reached the door and turned back to Symphony. "You know, Symphony, you owe nothing to anyone, but yourself. This is *your* life, it's not worth it unless you're happy."

Symphony had a feeling the woman was trying to tell her something, but didn't have the energy to decipher the code at the moment. She rubbed at her face and prayed she looked better than she felt, as she waited for Kyle Dean and his blasted rainbows.

Chapter 9

Kyle walked into the room, looked around at the shelves lined with books and then locked his eyes on the woman propped up in the corner of the sectional. Her lids were closed as he strolled towards her and took a seat on the ottoman next to her. He sat there staring at her as if he didn't know what to do or say. And maybe he didn't.

"What're you doing here?" The words slid out on the back of a long sigh. Her eyes were still closed so she didn't see the ghost of a smile that touched his lips. She could feel his comforting presence sitting next to her and reminded herself that he was practically a stranger.

"Gloria told me you wanted to see me." His words were guarded. "Was she mistaken?" He picked up one of her hands and she easily remembered the way he'd held her on the pier and the tender kisses that could definitely be an overture to a fiery concerto.

Heat tinted her cheeks.

"You're either angry that I'm here, or remembering how you wanted to kiss me earlier on the pier."

Symphony

She took in a quick sharp breath when she opened her eyes and brought him into focus. He'd removed his tie and jacket and the top button of his shirt was undone. Mercy, this man was handsome. His floppy blond hair kissed and highlighted by the sun was adorable on him. There was a sexy contrast of the tailored suit and untamed hair. It made him appear virile, sophisticate, and rugged.

"Why are you here?" She asked again and noticed the frown take shape on his face. He looked so endearing when he frowned. "You don't really know me, I was rude to you at the airport, I had a complete meltdown on you earlier...wait..." she began looking around. "What time is it anyway?"

"It's only about 2:30."

The service was at noon, so not too much time had passed, she thought.

"As I was saying...I had a complete meltdown on you earlier, and then I passed out. So I ask you again, why are you here?" She pulled her legs in under her and waited for his reply.

"You needed a friend."

"But you don't even know me."

"I know that you make the best pastries I've ever eaten. I know that you love coffee and you hate rude people who keep interrupting you while you're trying to drink it." His voice softened. "I know you've just lost someone dear to you and you've traveled here alone. I know that you're good and care about others." There was a pause and his eyes darkened. "And I know you taste sweet."

Symphony eased her hand from his. The contact, him sitting there looking like the definition of sexy, and his playful voice laced with the promise of something wicked, was too much to take in at once. Plus, he smelled so damn good. She wanted to place her head on his shoulder again just to inhale him.

He lifted a brow and put his hands on his thighs. "I also know that Terry Phoenix is someone from your past or someone who does or once meant a lot to you."

There was no sense in playing coy or pretending she didn't know what he was talking about. "Yes."

He nodded. But there wasn't anything in his face to give away what he was thinking at that moment.

"I also know that I'm sitting here and he's not." Just a touch of conceit puffed from beneath his collar. She wanted to roll her eyes. Men! But she smiled instead, because he was absolutely right, he *was* here and not Terry.

"How're you feeling Symphony James?"

"Much better. I'm sorry about all of this."

"Did you do it on purpose?"

She gave a soft chuckle. "No Sir, I have better ways of getting my kicks."

"Oh yea?"

That got his attention. She had no idea why she'd said that, except that she'd read it in a novel recently. What kicks? There hadn't been any kicks for about eight months. Not since she and Eric stopped hooking up. There was only work and creating delicious things for people to eat. She was dessert. The best part of the meal. The part that people sometimes skipped the meal to get to. To her, right now, it was enough.

Her cheeks heated and she was sure the tell-tell tinge of built-in rouge was apparent, "I mean, this was not my idea of fun. Embarrassing myself in front of people."

"Are you sure you're ok?"

"I'm fine. Just overwhelmed, not enough rest, and I hadn't eaten today."

"Well let's remedy that right now."

He hurried from the seat taking purposeful strides to the door before she could say anything. The door shut behind him and she took a moment to take a few deep breaths and to get her heart rate back to normal. Symphony felt so anxious around him—like a school girl with a crush on the basketball star. She wanted to get to know him and that scared the hell out of her. And what was she going to do about Terry? She knew she couldn't avoid talking to him forever.

Symphony noticed she was still in her dress from the funeral. It was a simple black sheath dress with capped sleeves. Thinking of the dress's purpose, she was suddenly doused with a fresh wave of sadness. It lay on her like buckets of old raw meat—cold, wet, and fetid.

As if restrained in a straight jacket, she suddenly felt uncomfortable and confined like the thin material was suffocating her—chocking her with the stench of grief.

Was this the moment when all her carefully tossed balls she'd juggled for so long, came crashing down on her? Was it finally time for her reality to meet the edge of her nightmares? Was she going to either wake up or just slip quietly into manufactured darkness?

She grabbed at the fabric around her middle. There was such a strong need to rip herself out of it, to fling off the acrid taste of grief. She felt maybe she was finally blissfully insane after seemingly teetering on the edge of it for such a long time. The dress suddenly felt heavy—too weighted down. Too everything.

Reaching for the zipper in the back, her hands were too shaky to remove the delicate eyelet hook. Frantically, she pulled at the zipper, without progress. Symphony stood, ignoring the slight sway of the room. She had to get out of the damn thing. It was narrow at the waist and would never go over her head. Frustration pushed hot tears from her eyes and a garbled scream that hurt her throat sent Kyle running back into the room. She felt as if someone was attacking her. Symphony saw Kyle stop just inside the doorway.

"Get me out of this thing!" She yelled as she fought with the dress.

He hesitated only a second, ran to her, and quietly stilled her hands. "Shhhh...I have you...I have you..." He repeated like a mantra.

She shook as he undid the clasp and unzipped the dress. She reached up and snatched it free from her shoulders and then down her body. She kicked it away from her like it was a poisonous snake. Kyle held her tightly, her back against his front, and arms down at her sides. For a moment, she let him and then reached for the straps of her bra like she was swatting away fire ants. Her shoulder's and area around her collarbone were red with welts and scratches.

"Hold on…I got it." He unfastened the bra quickly. "You're going to hurt yourself." He turned her towards him and shielded her body with his.

She felt safe.

She felt sane.

Stepping out of the hallway after slipping on a t-shirt and yoga pants, her standard lounge attire, she saw Kyle moving around the kitchen making a plate for her. His coat and tie were slung across one of the chairs at the breakfast table. It struck her again that she was here, alone with a man she hardly knew. Though fear was the farthest thing from her mind and she didn't really want to contemplate why he was here.

He turned and saw her watching him.

"You need to eat." Was all he said.

"Ok." She smiled. "I agree."

He turned back to what he was doing and she moved towards the the stools at the kitchen island.

After taking something for her headache and eating the food Kyle had so thoughtfully fixed for them, she felt like her old self again. Well… that wasn't really accurate. She no longer felt like her old self. She felt light and hopeful. Hopeful of what, exactly, she was still unsure.

There was no lingering awkwardness following her erratic display and him helping her strip out of her clothes. They'd moved around and talked as if it was a common occurrence for him to rescue a woman from flesh-eating, mind-altering, dresses.

"So, Kyle Dean what's your story?" She asked after they'd taken a seat on the wicker lounger on the patio. Aunt Helen had a thing for sectionals. Other than baking, she'd loved to read, and wanted comfortable places to be able to relax and enjoy her books—hence the sectionals.

He stared at her for a long time and she was sure he wasn't going to answer her question. Pain clouded his face and she was sorry she'd asked.

"I'm sorry, I didn't mean to pry."

He turned from her and she watched as he looked out over the water. She followed his lead watching the boats pass and wondered more about him.

"I was a combat photographer in the Army." She turned back to him—his voice impassive. He didn't look at her. He spoke to the wind. "We had incoming." She wasn't quite sure what he meant by that, but didn't want to interrupt him to ask.

He was in the Army?

Symphony

Somehow, she couldn't picture him in the Army with his blond floppy hair and cartoon t-shirts.

"A bunch of us were in the recreation tent and began to scramble for weapons and to determine what was going on out there. The camp was a temporary site near a small village. We were there to help with the construction of the school." She was surprised; she didn't know the soldiers helped with stuff like that. "I remembered I'd left my camera and my memory cards that had some very important shots on them, at my computer in the tent where our offices were housed."

Symphony could feel her heart beating faster. She knew this story would not end well and wanted to stop him from continuing. She didn't want him to renew old wounds, but somehow she felt as if he needed to release the demons he was holding inside. If this helped him, she would let him continue.

"There were people running everywhere. Didn't they know that by attacking us, they were also attacking their own people nearby?" The question went unanswered.

"The day before, I'd met a sister and brother. They were five and twelve—Umniya and Anah, orphans living in an abandoned building. Anah told me his named meant, answer. It fit him well, because he loved to ask questions. I couldn't wait for the school to

Symphony

be built so he could get as many answers as his head could hold."

"I grabbed my camera, stuffed the cards in my pocket and ran for the village, suddenly thinking about Uminya and Anah." He didn't say anything for a long while and then he finally turned to her, eyes pleading for understanding. "I was pinned in the corner of a bombed out office building and suddenly the bombing stopped. The quiet was almost as frightening as the bombs. Then I heard something. I immediately knew it was a soldier pleading for his life." His eyes closed as if he was in pain and he turned back to the water. "I crawled to an opening in the building, and there, on the ground, surrounded by three armed men, was my buddy, Harris." Kyle looked at Symphony. "Harris was expecting a baby at any moment and was due to leave Iraq in a week. It made me so anger that I literally saw red.

Harris couldn't die. Not like this. Not without seeing his son, holding him, watching him grow, and being the parents he and his wife talked about all the time. I pulled out my weapon. Harris spotted me and flatted himself in the dirt. I discharged the rounds and grabbed my camera hanging around my neck. I wanted Harris and everyone else to see the bastards who'd tried to steal his future from him, dead."

114

Symphony couldn't move. She just stared, eyes wide, grateful that he'd saved Harris.

"Furry still obscured my vision as I snapped the grisly scene. It took only seconds. I grabbed Harris who was in shock, and got him back to camp. Fortunately, there were no casualties on our side. I never got a chance to look for Anah and his sister."

"Days later," he continued, still looking her way, but seeing the scene from his past. "I was given an award for my bravery. It wasn't until after Harris left to go on leave that I was going through the pictures I'd taken since arriving to help with the school. There were lots of shots of the soldiers working on the building, some of the children and other villagers, and lots and lots of images of Anah and his little sister, and then," his words faltered and his voiced dropped to a gruff whisper, "I got to the shots from the day of the bombing. I truly had forgotten I'd taken them. It had been and impulse. I was not myself, but still, I made myself look at the inhuman monsters who'd tried to take my friend… and lying there…" He struggled for the words. "Lying there with a bullet through his head, was sweet, little, inquisitive Anah."

Angrily, he stabbed the air with his words, "I was awarded a medal for killing a kid." Then softer he spoke with a question in his tone, "For killing a kid? That's bravery?"

Symphony reached over and grabbed one of his hands and squeezed. "You did what you had to do to save, another soldier, to save his wife from grief, to save his son from growing up without him... I'm sure if you'd known who was holding the gun, you would've hesitated, a beat too long and Harris would've been dead...Possibly, you too."

"I've never picked up a camera again."

Chapter 10

Neither said anything for a very long while. They just watched the late afternoon turn into early evening. The sun behind them, leaving an unshielded view of the ocean meeting the sky. There wasn't anything specifically spectacular about it. No vivid colors—just the gray hue of the ocean joining the nondescript blue of the sky. Yet, even without the brilliancy of colors that people normally associate with the horizon, Symphony felt there's always a sort of a splendor that naturally goes along with the ocean and the heavens.

Symphony couldn't see herself living too far from the Atlantic. It was home—always had been. Even now, away from Florida, she still felt at home, because the Atlantic was at her front door.

Symphony thought back on when she first laid eyes on Kyle in the airport and wondered where he was from.

"Are you from Florida?" Symphony finally asked.

"Yes," Kyle turned towards her, "born and raised in Daytona." There it was—the beach-boy persona she'd seen in the airport.

117

"There's not too many native Floridians that I meet. Most people are transplants. Do you still live there?"

"Yep." He nodded proudly.

She felt a flutter of excitement knowing that he lived so close to her. "What brings you to South Carolina?"

An emotion she couldn't name, skittered across his face so quickly, she wasn't sure if she really saw it.

"I guess I can't say the beach, can I?"

"No." She laughed.

He turned back to the shore and then back to her as if he'd made some sort of decision. He looked absolutely delicious with his shirt unbuttoned at the top.

"I needed to disappear for a while." She was sure the question was plain own her face and was glad he didn't pretend not to see it. "My photo..." He clarified and seemed to inhale the entire ocean all at once. The sigh that followed was long and pregnant with a medley of heaviness. "The one with..." He paused again and Symphony instinctively knew which photo he was talking about. She reached over and placed her hand on his upper arm, slowly letting it travel up and down.

"It was one of the photos you took...after...you saved Harris." She wanted him to focus on the fact that

118

he saved a soldier's life—his friend, and not the fact that he'd shot the boy from the village.

He nodded. "All my life I've been wanting to get my pictures in Time Magazine…" A harsh laugh made her jump. "and that's the damn picture that gets in there."

She still didn't understand why he had to disappear for a while. Symphony had no idea what to say to him. The irony was cruel as it so often is in life. "How did they get it?"

"My command." He said. "The camera belonged to the army, as well as any pictures I'd taken with it. I have my own cameras, of course, but I hadn't wanted to bring them for that particular mission."

She could understand that. The last time she priced a decent camera, it was way more than she wanted to spend and if she had, she definitely wouldn't have wanted it in a warzone. His camera, she was sure, was way more expensive than what she was willing to let go.

Symphony gently stroked his shoulders as if she'd comforted him this way for years. "I still don't understand why you had to disappear for a while."

Kyle shook his head in disgust. "Reporters! Local and national, have been calling me, coming by my apartment and job, to interview me about the photos and what took place there."

"Oh." She still had so many questions and wanted to know so much more about him, but she would let him reveal himself to her at his own pace. It struck her suddenly that one of her rules was no personal conversations, but something happened on the plane that'd made her forget about her rules—made her forget why she had the rules in the first place. Somehow, that didn't seem to bother her at all.

"I really don't believe the Army would've wanted those photos exposed." He said.

She thought it wouldn't be something to share with the world either, especially in light of all the terrorist activity going on in the world right now. "I think," he continued. "it was leaked by an outside source. There're so many civilians working with our troops in the Middle East, from all over the world."

"So you came here to get away from reporters?"

"Yea." He answered, nodding his head.

"For how long?" She had no idea how long she would be in South Carolina and wondered if he would be staying as well.

"Couple weeks…a month. I don't know." He looked so defeated, she felt pained.

How could this be?

How could she take on the hurt of a man she hardly knew?

Kyle stood. "Come. Walk with me." And just like that, she noticed, the past no longer seemed to smother him. He extended his hand to her and she took it. "Show me around the island."

Symphony

"There's nothing really to show. Just the house... there's a trail over there that leads to the other property." She pointed near a stand of trees that looked to be an entrance to a magical forest. "And another that just travels the perimeter of the island." The other property, she thought, was where Terry was probably staying. She still couldn't believe he was there on Gwenda Island.

"And your aunt didn't mind living so isolated and alone?"

Symphony, thought again of Floyd Jenkins and wondered how often her aunt had really been alone.

"Oh, it's not so isolated. It's just a few minutes by boat to Charleston. There's a charter that'll come out when called or scheduled. Kind of a water taxi. And Aunt Helen has a boat of course." The realization that Aunt Helen was gone, and she no longer had anything, slowed her feet and stole her words.

Kyle noticed the change in Symphony, stopped and tuned to her. He pulled her gently into him and held her firmly. She allowed herself to be held by this man—again. And again, she didn't want to be any place else. After a time, he eased away from her, but not by much. He tucked a lock of her hair behind her ear and traced a finger down the side of her face.

"You know...the first time I saw you, you had this same look on your face, and just like then, I want to make whatever caused you to look like this, to go away."

Symphony

She gave him a slip of a smile. It was all she could manage. He was so sweet. Why him? Why was he able to get through all of her carefully placed defenses when no one else had since college?

And why was she letting him.

"I know there's nothing I can do to bring your aunt back," he said, "but I can hold you. I can be here. I can be your strength when you have none and I can wipe away your tears, until you know that crying doesn't mean you're defeated." He pushed a tear away with his thumb. "It's simply a release and I'll be here to catch you, if you let me." He palmed her cheek. She leaned in to it.

Lord help her.

Looking up at him, into his intense blue eyes, she whispered, "Why would you want to?"

"How could I not?" She recognized they barely knew each other, but the sincerity in his words told her that he would not only do all he'd said, but he would do it gladly.

"My life is such a mess right now." She thought about Cooper Read, Terry Phoenix, all the stuff she'd inherited, and…her losing her aunt—the rock in her life.

"I don't mean to be cynical, but that's never going to change."

She cocked her head slightly, but before she could ease her hand onto her hip, he lifted his mouth into an indulgent smile and traced the outline of her lower lip with such a feather-like touch, she wasn't sure if it was his touch or just the idea of it that was making sweet heat ripple through her. The sassy retort was swiped away.

"Symphony…"

Her name, a prayer on his lips. A litany pushing into the atmosphere and straight through her. It was almost enough to snap her poised control.

She nearly melted into a puddle.

"Yes?" The single word no longer held the fire she'd felt after his statement.

"You're taking my words wrong." Although her hackles were no longer up, she wanted to hear his explanation. "I didn't say that to upset you. I just want you to know that no one ever thinks their life is perfect and the ones who do, are lying to themselves. We just have to be happy with what we have."

His lips were moving, but all she could think was, why did she want to kiss him so badly? She wanted him to let her lose herself in his kiss. If he would just shut up, pull her close, and trail his lips along her neck, the conversation would be so much better. She thought about how much more they could say without saying anything at all.

An image of Terry showing up that last night, popped uninvited in her mind. She shook her head to rid herself of the memory.

"Symphony?" This time it was a question. His mouth suddenly grinning at her. And again she'd been caught ogling him. She rolled her eyes and turned to continue their walk. First, to rid herself of Kyle's imaginary kisses and also, because perplexity rattled her. All the energy she spent on Terry was exhausting and she was tired of being tired.

Kyle stood watching her walk away from him. She turned suddenly needing to lash out at something…someone. Anything that would help release her frustrations.

"Hypocrite!"

He frowned. "Huh?"

"You're a hypocrite!" She threw back at him with a haughtiness that belied her true feelings. Inside she was melting like wax in the Sahara and had no idea how to stop it.

Both hands on her hips and feet apart, she tried like hell to bring some clarity and control back to the situation, if that was possible. "Yes, you, Kyle Dean are a big fat hypocrite." She punctuated each word by stabbing the air with her index finger. His face was impassive. "You stand there spouting off about being happy with what you have." She threw her hands in the air. "Well, news break, Mr. Happy-Go-Lucky, you have a photo in freakin' Time Magazine, but are you happy with that realization? Nooo-o…you're hiding away pretending you're not as fucked up as me and everyone else!"

Those last words tumbled out of her mouth and fell flat at her feet, staring up at her with stinging accusation and indignation.

He said nothing. She felt horrible.

Horrible, horrible, horrible.

Symphony

Symphony closed her eyes and raked her hand through her hair. She already felt wild and untamed, so who cared if her hair matched. She stood there like that for several seconds and when she opened her eyes, he was still there. He was still there and the indulgence in his eyes made her feel even more like a bitch, because she knew that he didn't think she was, even though he'd called her one on the plane.

"You're right." He said, easily.

"No…" She shook her head. "No, Kyle. I'm sorry. I was out of line."

He extended his hand again. "Come on. Let's go for that walk."

"Kyle?"

"Com'on." He wriggled his hand around. "Do you want my arm to fall off?" He said in a slow deep octave.

Symphony tilted her head and squinted at him a bit. "Lady Sings the Blues?"

"You don't think that's my own line?"

"No." She said, unable to keep the smile out of her voice.

"And why not?"

"Because I've seen that movie a thousand times. My aunt was a big fan of Billy D. Williams."

"Busted."

"What do you know about some Billy D?

"What? A white boy can't watch 'Lady Sings the Blues?'"

She took his hand, rolled her eyes, and grinned. "Come on, Kyle Dean, let me show you Gwenda Island."

Chapter 11

After a fitful sleep, dreaming of the boy soldier Anah, Symphony uncoiled and relaxed in the rich aroma of her coffee, grateful for the robust flavor with its hint of spice. She needed it after very little sleep. She vowed to take the boat out later, anchor it in the middle of nothingness, and get some rest while the subtle rock of the waters lulled her to sleep.

It was 7am, later than she normally was up, but she didn't want to think about the day ahead. So, while the sky stretched and yawned awake, she took in the spacious kitchen facing the pier, and thought of Aunt Helen. Aunt Helen had been the rebel in her family, doing just the opposite of what her parents wanted her to do.

She'd left Charleston after finishing high school, defying her parents who'd wanted her to marry the preacher's son. However, she'd had dreams of owning her own bakery, so moved to live with her much older sister Ruth and her husband in St. Augustine, FL. Symphony learned later that Ruth's husband owned a large manufacturing company in St. Johns County, Florida and was extremely wealthy.

127

Symphony

Determined to make her own way, Helen went to a business college and worked in a restaurant called Mama's, that catered to many of the tourists visiting the town for its rich history and beaches. St. Augustine is the oldest city in the nation and attracted many visitors throughout the year. So, when people began to seek out the restaurant as one of the places to visit while in town, because of their exceptional desserts, Helen knew it was time to strike out on her own. She started with a little stand near the lighthouse. It didn't take long for people to learn that Helen's Bakery hosted the same baker as Mama's. Soon she was able to open a full-sized bakery, with several satellite locations in the region.

There were companies interested in buying the recipes of quite a few of her desserts, but she always refused. She didn't want her hard work massed produced in a factory. She wanted to keep what people paid for—baked goods made from the heart.

Symphony felt the same way. She still used some of her aunt's recipes, but most of them were her own, and she didn't want them massed produced all over the country. She wanted to maintain the integrity of her desserts. Her brand was special and she wanted the people of St. Augustine to feel special knowing Symphony's was something they could only get at home. Convincing Cooper Read of that was another story all together.

Thinking of Cooper Read, prompted her to call Ian to check on things. He advised her that Cooper was still refusing to take no for an answer, but Ian was sure he could handle him. He also assured Symphony that he was managing things well. Sells were steady and he and Ricco were handling the products for the store and catering orders.

Symphony had an additional crew who worked with her for special catering events. It was something Ian took care of normally, so there was nothing to be concerned about there. Although, Cooper Read did, in fact, concern her. He was known for getting what his clients wanted, and sometimes through unscrupulous means; she knew he was someone to watch. But for now, she would let Ian take care of things. He was more than capable, and extremely loyal.

Symphony again wondered how her life had changed in such a short time. She once remembered her aunt saying, "Baby, change doesn't wait until you're ready for it. It just knocks on the door, if you're lucky, and says 'I'm here!'" She would give her a wink that said, "Trust me on that."

Symphony smiled at the memory and took a sip of her piping hot coffee. Just then, Symphony was nearly startled out of her seat when she heard a knock on the patio door behind her. Coffee sloshed out of her cup, burning her thumb.

"Shit!"

She grabbed the worn kitchen towel her aunt used so often and pressed it on her hand. She turned around knowing instinctively that it was Kyle. He always seemed to know when she was enjoying a drop of coffee. It was his duty, it seemed, to not let her.

She turned and glared at the door, which was all glass, not giving a damn that it was rude. She held her coffee mug up and turned her back to him. He would have to wait. She had not invited him and it was seven freaking a.m.! She sipped her coffee, but couldn't suppress the smile that begged her mouth to turn up.

He knocked without a pause.

Knock, knock, knock, knock, knock, knock, knock...

She turned. He stopped.

"Kidnappings do not happen at convenient times, Symphony." His voice muffled, squeezing through the seam of the door and frame. She rolled her eyes and stood. Walking to the door she snatched it open, the other hand on her hip.

Symphony

His eyes widened, taking in her state of dress up close. Her nipples were apparently trying to reach through the soft fabric of the short nightgown. She could feel them tightening. Symphony crossed her arms over her chest.

"What are you doing here so early?"

"You're a baker; this isn't early to you." He threw back at her with that playful grin of his. He was right of course. This was not early to her at all.

He filled her door with masculinity and his scent was waking her up more than her coffee ever had.

"This is not a normal hour to call on folks. Especially those who are in mourning."

He paused a moment and stared at her. His eyes twinkled, but she was determined to remain stoic. "'Call on folks?' What are you, eighty?" But before she could give him the retort that was burning her tongue, he placed a finger over her lips.

Her eyes blazed at him again, but only for a moment, because the next instant he replaced his finger with his lips, and God help her, she couldn't remember her name.

Sweet sprinkles of heat melted her to the spot. The kiss was soft and brief, but oh my, she wanted more. She wanted him to fold her into him and hold her there. She remembered the comfort of his arms from yesterday on the pier. He was masculinity personified and she feared she was becoming addicted to him. Like her customers savoring the last flake of her croissants, she wanted him to melt on her tongue until she relished the last tiny bit, and still, she was sure she would beg for more.

With the force of a wrecking ball, she realized she wanted Kyle Dean. She wanted him to help her get out of her clothes, but more than that. She wanted the waves to rock her as she rode him in the middle of the ocean on a sailboat. She wanted to explore, taste, and suck every sun tanned inch of him.

This man could not be a casual sex partner. She knew it like she knew her name was Symphony Blaire James. He would get under her skin, into her veins, and infect her heart. Like in war, in love, there were always casualties. She didn't want to be one again.

"Ok?" She heard him ask.

Had he said something? How could a kiss so innocent, leave her mindless? This man was dangerous to her senses.

"I'm sorry, what did you say?"

He grinned at her, knowing his kiss stupefied her. "I said, from what you've told me about your aunt, she wouldn't approve of you sitting in this house or anywhere else, moping for the next few days. So, I thought we'd go hit some balls today."

Of course he was right about her aunt, but still...

Was it even proper?

She dismissed the question immediately, knowing what her aunt would say to that. Proper, to her, was whatever felt right.

Symphony's phone rang. She frowned, worried, because she knew Ian would only call her if there was a problem. "Hello!...Ian!" She could hear background noises but the caller didn't say anything. Pulling the phone from her hear, she saw that the number was unfamiliar. "Hello." She waited a few moments. "I guess they had the wrong number." Speaking to no one in particular, she placed the phone back on the counter. She turned back to Kyle, still standing in the doorway. "Hit some balls?" She finally asked. What in the world was he talking about?

"Yes, at a private range I know of." She was still confused. "May I come in, Symphony?" Her manners had definitely been tested over the last few days. She was sure her aunt was giving her the side-eye saying, *"Now Symphony Blair, that's not how we treat guests."*

She moved to the side to let him enter.

"Want coffee?" She asked with a tilted grin. He shook his head no. "Will you please explain to me what you're talking about? Hit some balls?"

"Yes, golf balls."

She then took in his attire, he was wearing khaki shorts and a white polo, looking kind of Tiger Wood-ish. "You play golf?"

"I was on my way to play professionally until…" His voice trailed off and then he asked her again. "So, will you join me? I woke up with a hankering to hit some balls this morning."

Her brows raised. He was going to play professionally? "Until what?"

His features hardened. "Until my best friend was killed in this so called war against terrorism."

She frowned. "I don't understand. How did that keep you from going professional?"

"I was pissed as hell. My best friend had gone off to fight in a war without me and those bastards had killed him. So, I joined the Army, because I wanted to somehow make a difference."

She knew how that had ended. He'd spent ten years in the Army with a couple of tours in the Middle East, fighting in a war that could've possibly left him broken.

"Oh." What else could she say?

This man had given up his dream of playing professional golf to fight for his country. Kyle Dean had depths to him that she wondered if she would ever truly know. But she knew she wanted to at least get to know him as much as she could while she could. If for no other reason than, because he was fun to be around.

"Sure, but I've never hit a golf ball in my life, so naturally I have no clubs. Ironic, since I live on a golf course. I also have another appointment with the lawyer soon and I don't know when I'll be free."

"No problem, I'll take care of you."

She was sure he was talking about helping her hit the balls and providing the clubs…and it was not unlike what he'd said when he helped her out of the flesh-eating dress…but….

Their eyes held for a long moment communicating what neither were ready to say or hear.

Symphony didn't need someone to take care of her. She'd been taking care of herself for a long time, but the honesty of his words, spoken with such conviction, cocooned her.

She almost wanted to see just how he would.

"By the way," he said, "which course do you live on?"

"I live in one of the newer communities near the World Golf Village."

He just stared at her. "Really?"

"Yea, why?"

"Oh, nothing…just thinking about the irony."

"Do you play there?"

"All the time." He almost sang the words.

She looked at the time on the microwave and turned quickly back to him, mentally ticking off the things she had to do to get ready for her day.

"How 'bout I meet you in Kiawah when I'm done. I can call you when I'm heading your way, but it may not be until after lunch. I have the sailboat."

He raised a brow. "I'm impressed. You sail."

"I do."

"Ok, I'll try to keep myself busy until you're done with your business."

"Don't be so impressed by my sailing. It's the least of my many talents… and I'm a master sailor." She said with a wink.

Chapter 12

Symphony had a dilemma. The paltry pile of clothes tossed across the bed may as well have been a flashing neon light that read, "NO SOCIAL LIFE." Her wardrobe was made for the kitchen and comfort. Her clothes had never been an issue before and she quietly wondered why she was worried about it now, although, she knew why. She just didn't want to admit it to herself.

On the bed was a mixed-matched assortment of slacks, shorts, a skirt, and a pair of jeans. She would have to go shopping for outfits. She had no idea how to dress for her meeting with the lawyer and hitting golf balls. She thought about bringing a bag with a change of clothes, but that seemed to scream, "TRAMP." Maybe she was putting way too much thought into it.

"Think of it like you're going to the gym," she told herself. "It's just a change of clothes."

The knocking on the door followed by the ringing of the bell, pulled her from the wardrobe crisis. Kyle was persistent, if nothing else, she thought. She wondered why he'd returned. Symphony turned the corner from the hallway, into the kitchen and dining area at the back of the house and stopped.

Symphony

She knew he would come, even though, a few times since yesterday she tried to pretend that she'd just imagined seeing him since he'd been so heavily on her mind lately.

But there he stood.

Her past, clad in dark jeans and a pink short-sleeved pullover that showed off how time had agreed with him. Six years had chiseled him into a more handsome, finer version of his college self.

Terry Phoenix, though he was handsome, his attraction was in his whole presence. He walked and even stood with an air of confidence, yet there were times she'd wished he'd exuded more. Since college, he seemed to stand a little taller. Looking through the glass of the patio door, his eyes held hers and she couldn't discern what he was thinking.

Somehow, Symphony put one foot in front of the other and propelled herself towards him. His face was impassive, but his eyes never strayed.

Inside, her body shook. Taking a deep steadying breath, she turned the knob and was once again sharing space with the only man she'd allowed her heart to love.

"Hi." She said.

"Hi." He replied.

She stepped back to let him in, trying to steel herself.

From what, she wasn't exactly sure.

She had no idea what any of this would do to her.

Why was he here?

What did he want?

Why now, of all times, to show up?

She saw him looking around.

"Nice place."

Sighing, she replied, "Thanks." Symphony walked over to the breakfast table and gestured for him to sit. "You know how I feel about small talk. Why are you here, Terry?"

He gave her a half grin and damn it, why did he have to do that.

No.

No.

She mentally shook her head.

No. She would stay poised and controlled. But as she remembered their unspoken goodbye, her body was weak and disobeying.

Symphony shook her head and looked at him expectantly.

His voice low and even. "How're you feeling? I was worried about you yesterday."

Symphony

"I'm fine. I hadn't been eating and sleeping properly, and well…my aunt." And you, she thought, but kept that part to herself. "I'm fine now." She waited for him to answer her question. She also wanted to ask him so badly how'd he'd been, but didn't really think she could stand knowing.

"The guy…the guy at the funeral…is he someone special to you?"

She stared across the table at him. Not because she didn't want to answer the question, but rather, she didn't know how to answer it. *Was* Kyle someone special? She didn't know. She liked him, sure, but…

Obviously, Terry took her silence as affirmation. His eyes narrowed a touch. Disappointment, deep and accusing sprang at her and silence stretched across the room.

Why was this so difficult? And what the fuck was that look for?

"Do you love him?" He asked, flatly.

Silence.

Lifting her chin, she shot back, "I don't see how that's any of your business, Terry."

"Oh, but it is."

Irritation clawed at her from just looking at the glint in his gaze and the condescending tilt of his smile. She looked at the time. She didn't have time for this and what did he mean by that? "Look, I have an appointment shortly. Why are you here?"

Why did that question prompt a smile from him, *again*?

He rubbed his hands along the tops of his thighs underneath the table. "I'm here for my cousin's wedding reception. Imagine my surprise when your name was mentioned." His voice softened, dropping low and laced with sincerity. "Gloria told me about your aunt and I wanted to be here." He paused. "I'm so sorry for your loss. I had to see you, Symphony."

She would be lying to herself if she didn't wonder if he was seeing someone. Will there be someone on his arm at the reception? Her eyes darted to his hand before she could stop them.

"No, I'm not married." He spoke as if it was what he was thinking she was hoping to find out.

She didn't reply to that.

She stood, "It's nice to see you Terry. I hope you're doing well." He stood too, taking her cue that he was being dismissed.

They stood facing each other, an ocean between them and no space at all. She wanted to tell him to leave, but she didn't. She wanted to believe there was nothing still between them, but she couldn't.

She wanted to not react to the kiss that she knew was coming, but she didn't know how.

It was simple and complex. It was soft, tender, and greedy all at the same time.

It was Terry.

His head dipped down to hers, meeting her lips, expectant and receiving. His arms slid easily around her, pulling her close. They were familiar and safe... like home.

But she didn't live here anymore.

Six years, three months, and seven days, sober, and just like any addict, one hit and all those days were blown to hell. She tried to rationalize it in her head. Tried to tell herself that the kiss meant nothing, but the moment his oh so familiar lips connected with hers, she knew that was a lie.

She'd combusted into a vapor of steam, wishing somehow things could be easy and uncomplicated. Wishing that her aunt was here to give her advice. To help her understand what was going on in her life—with her emotions...with everything.

Terry smiled down at her, looking very pleased with himself. "Just as I thought." The words punctuating his arrogant expression.

She frowned and before she could try to stop them, tears filled her eyes and spilled over. Never had she been a woman prone to tears, not even as a little girl. She didn't like this new Symphony who cried at the drop of a hat. Her emotions had been so transparent lately. It was uncomfortable and it made her feel weak and vulnerable. Not liking that at all, she slapped the tears away and took a step backwards when Terry reached to touch her. Complete and total confusion and lack of control was getting the best of her.

"You need to go." She told him.

"Symphony, I—"

"Go… please."

He looked at her, nodded his head in acquiescence and stepped passed her to the door.

He turned; her back was still to him. "It's still there, Symphony. I know you felt it. Just as I did."

She couldn't move. All she knew was she couldn't ride this merry-go-round. It was fun and exciting, but it led to nowhere. She let out a breath she didn't know she was holding when she heard the door shut. Turning, she watched him climb into a Jeep and drive away.

Symphony touched her lips, still reeling from the kiss. "Damn him." She whispered.

Chapter 13

Symphony eventually settled on a pair of tan capris pants and a sleeveless soft green collard polo. She figured there wasn't a need to dress up to see the lawyer. It wasn't like she was going to court or anything, plus the last time she'd met him, he was in a shabby oversized worn brown suit. There'd been a shine to the suit like it had been ironed dirty.

Apparently, Mr. Samuels Jr. was the son of the late Mr. Samuels, whom her aunt had done business with. To be honest, she didn't like the looks of him and hoped their business wouldn't last long.

He had contacted Gloria to give Symphony the message of their meeting today, saying he'd misplaced her number. That didn't bode well either, she thought.

Symphony looked at her watch. The appointment was at 10:30. It was now 10:42. Frustration, irritation, and just plain old ticked nerves, made her jump as the creaking door announced another visitor to the lobby of the office that had seen better days. It smelled of mold and she dared not sit too far back in the frayed upholstered chair. At one time it had been burgundy, perhaps, but was now pink and in need of a burial.

"Ms. James?"

It was the woman who'd just walked into the office.

"Yes?"

The woman clutched a leather briefcase with one hand and the other, she stuck out to Symphony.

"Hi, I'm Alexandra Phoenix. I'm sorry I'm so late." The woman looked around the room and then at her watch. "You're still waiting?" Her face tightened.

Confusion along with recognition of the last name, greeted Symphony.

Phoenix?

Who was this woman?

She was dressed impeccably, in a creamy yellow pantsuit that tastefully molded to her curves. Her hair was a golden bronze color just like Symphony's, in fact, they looked like they could be sisters, Symphony thought. Along with the suit, she wore an air of confidence that betrayed her petite size.

"Gloria asked me to meet you here to make sure everything is on the up and up."

"Gloria? ... Up and up?" Symphony stumbled through her words as she stood to shake this stranger's hand, who clearly had something to do with Terry's family.

They were everywhere.

Symphony

"Yes, I'm a lawyer." Alexandra smiled and her dimples made deep adorable wells in her cheeks. "I'm married to Gloria's stepson, Joshua."

Oh. Symphony remembered Terry talking about his cousins Joshua and Landon Phoenix. Their father owned the company he'd planned to work for. Symphony gave her a smile that was almost a mirror image of Alexandra's, though her dimples weren't near as deep. She stood a few inches taller than the stylish lawyer, but their resemblance to one another was remarkable.

"It's nice to meet you Mrs. Phoenix. Please, call me Symphony."

"And call me Alex. Is it ok that I'm here? To join you in your meeting, I mean."

"Yes, of course." Symphony was relieved to have someone on her side in something she knew nothing about. "Do you live here in Charleston?"

"I'm originally from Baton Rouge, Louisiana, but since Joshua and I've been married we float between Louisiana and Boston." She chuckled a bit and gestured for Symphony to retake her seat, although she looked hesitant about putting her light suit in the filthy chair.

Fortunately, she didn't have to, the receptionist announced that they could go in to see Mr. Samuels.

146

Symphony

When the women walked in, Lincoln Samuels was wiping away crumbs from his mouth and tossing the remnants of his meal in the trash can next to the desk. Both women looked at each other, knowing this fat bastard had made them wait past their appointment time to eat his breakfast.

"Mr. Samuels, I'm Alexandra Wyatt Phoenix. I'm Ms. James's representation."

The bushy brows on his portly face raised in surprise for the briefest of moments, but then tried to look unaffected by the announcement that Symphony had legal representation.

"I wasn't aware you had a lawyer, Ms. James." His bulging eyes looked at her accusingly. "We've only some loose ends to tie up." He walked around the desk that was far too eccentric for the drab décor and extended a clammy hand to them both. Symphony had to keep herself from reaching into her bag for hand sanitizer.

"Where are my manners?" he said, waving a hand to the seats facing his desk. "Wyatt...Wyatt?" His brows creased. "You wouldn't happen to be related to old Carl Wyatt, the environmental lawyer."

Alex crossed her legs and plastered a smile on her face, but Symphony could tell she liked this man less than she did.

Symphony

"Yes, Carl Wyatt was my father, Mr. Samuels."

"Call me Sonny, my dear."

"Call me Mrs. Phoenix, Sonny." In an instant, she was all business with no intentions of prolonging the meeting. "You mentioned loose ends?" Her head tilted and her eyebrow shot up like a weapon. Symphony liked Alex more and more. Sonny, on the other hand clenched his jaw, pointed his eyes to the mess on his desk, and began shuffling nervously through the papers lying there.

Since they were in town, the women decided to do a little shopping and were becoming fast friends. Symphony was enjoying herself with Alex. She'd never had a female friend, or any real friends. She now realized it was probably because she just figured anyone she let herself care about would eventually get tired of her and leave her alone, like her parents.

They found a little sandwich shop near Battery Park and stopped for a bite to eat. It was nearing noon, but the heat wasn't yet so stifling that they couldn't take advantage of the patio tables outside. The two women could see the people streaming in and out of the market for prime people watching.

Symphony

"Thank you so much, Alex. I knew Samuels was a creep, but I hadn't figured him on being a thieving one."

"It was my pleasure. It's jerks like him that give lawyers a bad name."

Lincoln Samuels or Sonny, hired a shady appraiser and land surveyor who basically lied by padding the worth of the land and house on Gwenda. Luckily, Gloria and Alex stepped in or Symphony would not have been the wiser. The more the property is worth, the higher percentage of fees the lawyer could claim from the estate.

"So how do you know Terry?"

Symphony had not been ready for the question. She stalled by toying with her sandwich. She picked off the pickles and rearranged her tomatoes to be more evenly distributed. "Why do they always stack the tomatoes in one spot like this?"

"I know what you're doing." Alex leveled at her. "It's ok if you don't want to answer."

Symphony was instantly relieved.

"But answer the question anyway."

She gave a soft chuckle. "I bet you're hell to your opponents in the courtroom."

Alex smiled. "I guess I could be, but I'm more of a behind the scenes type of lawyer. I just make sure the businesses Joshua and I run, stay legal."

"What types, of businesses?"

"I know what you're doing. Just know you won't get out of it." She gave Symphony a wry grin. "Actually I'm part owner of a couple nightclubs slash sports bars slash restaurants in New Orleans and Boston."

"Really?" Symphony never would've guessed that the little spitfire was a nightclub owner. "How did you end up owning a nightclub?"

"Well, it was actually all coincidence, really. I worked as a bartender while going through college as a suggestion from my advisor. She thought I was going to burn out if I kept up the pace of heavy course loads and constant studying. So, she suggested I find a job. I applied for the job, thinking there was no way they would hire an inexperienced girl as a bartender at a sports bar." Alex pointed to her chest. "I knew nothing about sports and nothing about drinks. I didn't even have my first drink until after I'd graduated and was on a date with Joshua." She shook her head at the memory.

Symphony was reeling. Alex not only looked like her, their lives had been quite similar. She went on to tell her that after she graduated, the sports bar burned down and she loaned the owner money to rebuild. She'd inherited money from her dad with the completion of her schooling. The owner refused to take the money unless she came on as a partner.

"And the rest, as they say, is history."

"Wow." Symphony was speechless for a moment, but then, had so many questions. "Why didn't you just hang out with your friends from school?"

"Had none."

"Why?"

"No time. My best friend had gotten married and moved away and anyway, I was too busy trying to be the lawyer my dad wanted me to be. I had some pretty big shoes to walk in."

"Yea, I was impressed that Samuels knew your father."

"I'm not surprised. Carl Wyatt was big on stepping on a lot of toes around the country. Especially for the cause of the environment. When you make as much racket as he did, people are bound to know you."

Symphony was in absolute awe. She could tell Alex still had a difficult time talking about her father. She knew she would be that way for a very long time, if not forever, when thinking about her aunt.

Symphony

For a while, the noises from the street and shoppers invaded their little space at the table. Symphony wondered what it would've been like to have a friend like Alex while growing up. She hoped she and the woman could continue to be friends.

Catching Alex shoving far too many chips into her mouth at one time, she leaned forward and said, "Terry Phoenix was the only man that has ever moved me." Symphony sighed and her eyes slid shut with the memories. "That is… until I met Kyle Dean on the airplane flying up here."

Alex raised that razor sharp brow of hers and brought her hand up to her too stuffed mouth, too late to catch the chips flying out of it.

Chapter 14

"How can you hook your fingers like this and still swing straight? This feels weird." Symphony complained.

"I know, but that's how it's done. It won't feel weird after a while."

She was having a difficult time gripping the club in the way Kyle was directing her to hold it. Seemed to her that you should be able to hold it without having to hook your pinky onto your index finger. But what did she know, he was the expert.

Here, let me show you. Kyle moved to stand behind Symphony. He placed his hands on her waist and she inwardly cursed Terry Phoenix. Her body was on a heightened alert and sensitive to the touch, but unlike earlier when she'd nearly melted from Kyle's hands on her, they now felt awkward and invasive. She felt like pushing him away, but she didn't. Terry Phoenix did not control her body; she did—or at least that's what she kept trying to tell herself.

She finally got the hang of things and was able to get the balls to go where she wanted them, but the weird placement of her hands left her force a bit lacking.

"The difficult part is getting the ball to go where you want it. The distance will come after a while."

She could see why some people liked golf. Once you hit the ball just right and it did what you wanted it to, it was like a high you wanted to keep trying to get over and over.

"So, are you going to tell me what's wrong or is it none of my business?"

She'd been putting the clubs back into the bag when he'd spoken. She looked up. "What do you mean?"

"I mean you seem to have a lot on your mind and something tells me it has nothing to do with the lawyer's office."

"You're so smart; what does it have to do with then?" Irritated again, by a man thinking they knew what was going on in her own head.

"You saw him today, didn't you?"

She looked away and put the last club in the bag. Symphony turned back to Kyle and knew she couldn't avoid the question. She knew who he was talking about.

"Yes."

"Do you love him?"

Symphony

Her head throbbed. Why was that the first thing both men had asked?

"He asked me that very question..." There was a pause and then she said, "about you."

"He asked if you loved *me*?" Kyle seemed surprised by that.

"Yea, I guess we looked like a couple."

"And your reply?"

"I didn't."

To say she was out of her element would be an understatement. She felt like fish trying to walk and all she wanted to do was to go back to her kitchen and bake. Her kitchen, her music, they were her only friends and until now, she'd thought they were enough.

They weren't.

She'd enjoyed hanging with Alex more than she could have imagined.

And Kyle...

Kyle Dean was a different story all together.

She'd lived life on her own terms, with the exclusion of anyone else, but her aunts and the few trysts she'd had throughout the years.

They weren't enough.

Symphony had no idea how to interact with others socially or how to deal with the complexities of relationships. Not on these terms, which had no terms

155

at all. Not everyone went around meeting people with a list of "no this and no that."

Her rules had not served her well, so she suddenly decided not to use them. She would take Alex's advice and be honest, be happy, and most of all be willing to allow herself to live with the consequences of her choices.

Kyle eyed her, but he didn't say anything else. He walked over to where she was standing. "Come, take a ride with me."

"A ride?"

"Yea. Com'on."

He reached for her hand and she took it without hesitation. She hadn't quite figured out where they were. He'd met her in Charleston where she'd left her aunt's boat docked there to ride with him. His was a small speedboat that cut through the water quite effortlessly. The ride wasn't excessively long, but it wasn't a quick ride either. She thought they were going to Kiawah where he told her he was staying, but instead, they'd traveled to a more secluded place.

She still wondered what he did for a living, because staying on Kiawah for up to a month wasn't in reach for the average layman. However, she put the thought aside for the moment as they climbed in a golf cart and drove away from the driving range through tall lush grass. He reached in a cooler placed near their feet between them and pulled out two bottles of water. She salivated at the sight, realizing she was thirsty. The sun did more than warm her skin; her right arm and leg felt like a giant ant had her underneath a magnifying glass. The cold water was nearly painful, it felt so good going down her throat. She wiped away the dribble of water that escaped to her chin, "Ahhh... that hit the spot," she beamed with a smile.

Kyle's eyes widened and a look of chagrin took over his features. "I'm sorry, why didn't you tell me you were thirsty."

"I wasn't until that exact moment."

They'd driven from the driving range that was located near the beach through knee high grass, leaving a distinct path as the cart traveled along. Kyle turned near a stand of trees and suddenly they were engulfed in near darkness. She turned to him, but before she could question anything, they were in another clearing. Looming large ahead of them was a two-story narrow building. She looked around trying to spy anything that would give her a clue as to where they were. She couldn't tell if they were on part of the mainland or if this was one of the many islands that dotted the coast of South Carolina.

"Are you in love with him?"

Symphony

The words floated softly enough to her, shrouded in something sweet, cloying, and sticky—something akin to cotton candy, and she was sure he had no idea of the Pandora's Box he was opening.

It was a simple question or should've been, but when the unassuming words made their way to her they attacked like cobwebs do to unsuspecting people who haphazardly walk into their intricately spun traps.

She wanted to fling the question away—to slap it into nonexistence. *Are you in love with him?* The words multiplied into infinity.

Her shoulders stiffened, she took in a deep breath, and quickly let it out before her entire posture sagged. Frustrated, annoyed, and defeated, Symphony dragged her eyes his way. He wasn't facing her. He stared straight ahead as if he'd just asked her if she wanted coffee or tea.

When Kyle pulled to a stop in front of the coral painted building, which she suspected was a house, he faced her—features guarded and serious. Under the blazing heat of the South Carolina sun, the crash of truth radiated loudly in her ears, but the answer was vague, penetrating, and opaque, like fog. She could feel its weight, see that it was there, she could smell the damp mist of it, taste its blandness like the flavor of a boiled egg white, but she couldn't capture it.

The truth and answer to that question left her flat, but she refused to be a slave to its indecisiveness.

Today—right now, she would answer him and be free of its grip.

Chapter 15

"I used to be, but not anymore." She stated with finality.

"Since when?"

She could've said it was none of his business, since truly it really wasn't, but something deep within her wanted it to be his business. *She* wanted to be his business. The kiss she and Terry shared earlier meant nothing, no matter what Terry thought. She wanted to be over him.

So, she would be.

She lifted her chin and held on to his eyes. "Since now." She couldn't tell if it was relief she saw or something else. "I have a question for you."

"Shoot." He replied with confidence.

"Why did you ask?"

"I wanted to know if a man had your heart."

"That's not what you asked." She tapped the empty water bottle against her leg. "You asked if I was in love with Terry."

He looked thoughtful. "You're right." He stepped out of the cart and waved to her. "Com'on…let's get out of this heat."

160

For some reason her heart began to drum faster in her chest. He stood there waiting for her. "We'll get the clubs later."

"What is this place?" She asked looking up at the intricate design of the eaves.

"It belongs to my friend, Mike. We used to play golf together."

"Is it a home?"

"Yes, he lives here."

She looked over at him. "Is he here now?"

"Nah…he travels a whole lot and left right after I got here. He's currently in Montana installing or maintaining a zip line in the mountains somewhere."

"That's what he does for a living?"

"Yep." He said digging in his pocket.

"What about you? What do you do for a living?"

"For now, I'm giving private lessons at a few golf courses near Daytona and Orlando."

"And beyond that?"

He didn't say anything, just produced the keys from his pocket and put one in the lock. He let her hand go and she wasn't sure if it was so he could open the door or if he was pissed by her question. "I only asked, because you said, 'for now,' as if there was something else you wanted to do."

He didn't respond.

She looked over to spot a bee flying near the top of his head. "Don't move, there's a bee—" Before she could say anything else, Kyle began waving wildly at the bee. Surely, his erratic behavior caused it to sting him on the hand. The entire episode was so comical that Symphony's mouth fell open and her eyes widened in shock at first, before she shook with laughter. Her hand on her chest and eyes squeezing shut at the hilarity of his actions.

When Symphony opened her eyes Kyle's swollen hand grabbed at his throat and his face turned an angry red. *Oh God, he can't breathe. He must be allergic to bees.* Her hands slammed the sides of her head and she stared dumbfounded at the scene unfolding in front of her. At a loss, she had no idea what to do.

"Kyle!" She was at his side a heartbeat later as he fell to his knees. Fear and panic gripped her so acutely that tears blurred her vision. "Kyle! Kyle!" She repeated. "What do I do?"

His eyes glazed at the cart as he pointed toward it. She figured his throat was closing, but he managed to get out the word "bag."

Symphony

Symphony's feet pounded the ground as she raced with all her might to the golf cart. She ran to the back of it.

Bag?

The golf bag?

She was about to start going through the pockets.

No!

She saw it. There was a small bag near the cooler up front that she hadn't noticed before. She stumbled when she rounded the cart and threw herself in to reach the mini blue backpack. The cooler tumbled over, spilling ice and water everywhere, herself included. She didn't have time to think about that. She grabbed the bag and looked back at Kyle who was now curling into a heap on the patio of the house.

"Oh God! No!"

Hands moving as fast as she'd ever seen them, she unzipped the bag and dumped the contents on the seat. A bottle of pills, a syringe and a rectangle box that read "EpiPen" fell out. She snatched the EpiPen with shaking hands and ran back to Kyle. When she reached him, he was nearly blue. She ripped open the box, jostling the pen in her hand, she looked at it and didn't have a clue what to do with it.

Symphony

Come on Symphony, get it together, you can do this.

Her heart felt too big for her chest; she could hear the pounding of it in her ears, and her head whirred with adrenaline pumping fast and furious through her. She quickly turned the thing and saw a picture of what to do. Thank goodness!

Symphony pulled off the blue safety release as instructed. She hovered the orange end over his thigh like it showed in the picture and nervously glanced at him. Kyle was no longer flailing about and she didn't have enough time to think if she was doing it correctly or not, she just pushed up the leg of his shorts and jabbed it into the side of his upper thigh.

Almost immediately, he began to cough and the blue coloring of his face was being replaced by the redness again. On her knees, wet from the cooler, sweat running down her face, and hovering over his thigh with the EpiPen still clutched in her hand, relief flooded through her.

Kyle gasped for air. She crawled towards him ignoring the harshness of the concrete biting into her knees and shins. "Kyle, are you ok?" Her voice shaking, she cradled his head in her lap. Looking down on him, she asked again. "Are you ok?" Absently, she began sliding her fingers through his hair. It was soft and silky. She briefly wondered if she was attracted to the novelty of dating a white guy, then dismissed the thought all together. She honestly hadn't thought about him being another race until they'd talked about the movie "Lady Sings the Blues," yesterday.

"Please don't tell me I have to lose consciousness for you to run your fingers through my hair like this again."

Symphony looked down at shining blue eyes. He was ok. "Thank God. You're ok?" She needed his reassurance. She'd never been so scared in her life. Resting on her heels with his head in her lap, she smiled at him and he smiled back. Their eyes spoke to the other. It was becoming a habit. One day she hoped to be able to understand the language.

Placing her hands on his cheeks, she asked again, "Are you ok, Kyle Dean?"

"I still think Symphony James Dean is a kick ass name."

"You're probably still needing oxygen to your brain." He smiled up at her. "Kyle!" She shouted, needing to know he was all right.

"Yes, yes. I'm fine." His eyes held hers again. They were clear and serious this time. "Thanks to you." She didn't say anything. "That's only the second time I've needed the EpiPen." She looked down at it still lodged in his thigh.

He must've felt it there, because he reached and pulled it out. She watched it roll away from them and stop just at the edge of the concrete patio. "You scared the hell out of me, Sir."

"I didn't die."

"No, you didn't." She agreed, softly.

They both smiled at each other again.

"So, do you think you can get up?" She asked.

"Do I have to?" He countered, burying his head into her lap. "Why are you wet?"

"The cooler. I knocked it over."

"Ok, let's get up...I should have some dry clothes for you to put on." He began to push himself up.

"What're you doing?" She pushed his shoulders back down. We've got to get you to the hospital.

"I'm fine."

"I just watched you nearly die on this porch. You're going to the hospital if I have to tie you up to do it."

"Ok...Ok." He slowly eased himself up and she did the same. "But, will you give me a rain check on tying me up?"

She rolled her eyes trying to dismiss the image of Kyle tied up beneath her, because he would definitely be beneath her while she did all manner of wickedness to him.

Chapter 16

They had opted to go to one of the many emergency centers instead of a hospital to expedite the process. The doctor told her that Kyle needed to be monitored closely for the next twenty-four hours. Symphony insisted he stay with her on Gwenda Island. He'd been given a heavy dosage of allergy meds which promptly knocked him out.

Right now, he was fast asleep in one of the guest rooms. She'd stuck her head in to check on him and couldn't help herself from walking into the room with her robe tied securely around her. She sat on the bed next to him, and gently stroked his head and face. He was lying on his side sleeping so soundly that he was not disturbed by the dip of the bed or her movements.

She'd been so frightened earlier. Tracing her finger lightly down the contour of his nose, he looked better than a Greek god, tangled in the sheets. She could easily see him running along the beach with a surfboard and then riding the waves that licked the shores of Florida.

Symphony

He was so different from Terry. She could never see Kyle in a boardroom or sitting behind a desk. Kyle seemed like a feral and free soul.

She envied that.

It was so difficult for her to be that way. It never occurred to her to wonder why. She woke up early so she could be the first person at work. She ran her business with exact precision like an orchestra. All the high and low points were conducted and they were that way, because it's how she wanted it—how she thought they should be.

The men in her life had a specific purpose. They fit neatly in a box with no tentacles to wrap around or suction themselves to her. There were never any surprises, no blurred lines—their arrangements clear and explicit. Since she'd met Kyle, all of that had gone to hell. Here he was in her personal space and for once she just wanted to be reckless and do whatever the hell she wanted, simply, because she could.

"Am I still dreaming or are you really here in bed with me." His voice was gravel, but not abrasive. It was an early morning or middle of the night sound. She loved the way it felt—a soft rumble caressing her ears.

"Yes, I was molesting you while you slept." She said, with no traces of humor on her face.

Symphony

"What fun is that?" He asked, turning to his back not bothering to pull the sheet and comforter over his naked chest.

"Hmm…It was fun for me." She clicked the side table lamp on and the soft light caused him to squint a bit. She tried not to pay attention to the room and furnishings that her aunt had so carefully decorated.

As if they had a mind of their own, her fingers traveled to the pink area that surrounded his tiny man buds. She wanted to take each of them between her teeth until he winced with a pleasurable pain.

"I bet I can top it." He countered with a seductive challenge.

She forced her gaze from his toned chest and tried to concentrate on his wellbeing, although her body was voting against it. "How're you feeling?"

"A bit foggy from the allergy meds, but other than that, I'm fine." His features became very serious. "Thank you for today." He turned to his side to face her, his head near the side of her thigh and she instinctively reached to gently let her fingertips skirt along his jawline and then to absently stroke his hair. She loved the way it tickled her knuckles. He must've liked what she was doing because he let out a satisfying purr-like moan.

"Have you always been allergic to bees or is it something you developed later in life?" This simple contact with him, it was so, so, intimate. More intimate, she thought, than if they were lying there naked.

Why did she conjure that image? Desire blossomed and spread open like the soft petals of a rose in sunshine.

"Since I was about ten."

"Huh?" It took her a moment to realize what he was talking about. Oh, she suddenly remembered, his allergies. "Are you allergic to anything else?" She filled in quickly, not wanting him to notice her lack of attention on his words and note the intense consideration she was paying to his body.

"Nuts and spring."

"Spring?" She asked with an amused frown.

"Yea, from March until June, I pretty much live in a bubble or stay so loaded with allergy meds that I'm practically a zombie."

"I'm sorry I laughed at your bee antics."

His lips parted in a wicked grin. "What are you going to do to make it up to me?"

Not another moment to waste. Not another moment to wonder *what if* or *who* or *should I*. She pulled off the belt tied around her robe and the scarf she had tied onto her ponytail. "I'm going to tie your wrists to the headboard and ride you like a wild stallion until you can't remember what I should be apologizing for." She paused to take in his reaction to her words. His eyes widened with surprise and then darkened with exquisite anticipation. "And then I may let you taste some of the pastries I baked while you were knocked out...Ok?"

Kyle replied by rolling onto his back again and placing his hands behind his head. He licked his lips. She wasn't too sure if it was from the expectation of her or her pastries, but the spike of need that shot through her from his scandalous look was so intense, she captured his mouth and didn't plan to let it go until she'd gotten her fill of kisses.

Her mouth didn't hover or contemplate. It didn't leisurely close the distance between them; it rushed in eagerly, clanking teeth and tasting the tangy edges of his recent sleep, quickly masked by mutual desire and rash abandonment. She let her hand roam over his chest, feeling the thin downy hair in the center that she hadn't noticed just by looking. Finding his tiny tight nipple with her curious hand, she tweaked it hard, buoyed even further by his sharp intake of breath that she felt more than heard.

Symphony

Since Terry, Symphony made sure she was always armed against the tiny pieces of life that infiltrated the weak and bore into the heart, inflicting havoc on judgment, thoughts, and actions.

Kyle disarmed her.

Completely and without remorse.

He made the morning kiss that had rekindled her memories of times with Terry, burn away into nothing.

Only this, right now—only Kyle remained.

She was tired, tired of being the stone—unfeeling, without warmth, and alienated from life. She wanted to feel again. Even if it meant getting hurt. At least she'd know she was living.

Symphony broke the kiss, grabbed her bottom lip with her teeth, and slowly released it into a feline smile while rubbing her core against his muscled thigh. Oh how she wanted this man. Kyle lifted a bit and captured that same lip between his, sucking until he was swallowing her moans. His tongue licked, tasted, and tangled with hers. It was like he was trying to know every part of her.

And this was just the start.

Her womanly core expressed its yearning with a dull pulsating ache. Before she was completely lost to her desires, she lifted the covers so she could slide in with him. Sliding her leg over him, she centered herself so she could have easy access to spread his arms out and tie them to the metal spindles that made up the headboard. Although, Symphony was not prepared to have his ridged erection pressed between her legs. Her thin panties did nothing to shield her from it. The dull ache turned quickly into throbbing need. She nearly came apart from just the pressure of him smack center on her clit coupled with the kissing.

She had to slow this down.

Slow it *way* down.

His groan of protest gave her a delightful thrill when she broke the kiss to secure his arms. She wanted to feel his touch, yes, but the idea of tying him up and pleasuring him senseless was turning her on. She knew if he tested her readiness, he would find her slick and wet.

She tied the first wrist quickly, but on the way to the second one, she toyed with him. Her fingertips dallied from his shoulder to his hand. She played with his palm. Circling it with her index finger, he caught her by surprise when he linked their hands together.

"Symphony."

She saw the intenseness in his blue-eyed gaze. "Yes?"

"I just want you to know that being here with you...like this." He squeezed her hand with his free one. "It means a lot to me. I mean, I don't do casual flings...ever." His voice, soft, seductive, and serious. She raised her brows at this, but didn't say anything. How would he feel about her *only* doing casual flings? Was he trying to tell her something? Tell her that what they were about to share, what they were sharing now, would change whatever they were before this moment.

"What I'm saying is..."

"Shhh..." She placed a soft kiss on his lips.

"Symphony." The pads of his fingers stroked her face and threaded through her hair.

She didn't feel like this was the right moment for sensual confessions, but since he'd brought it up she would lay it all out there.

Chapter 17

Symphony sat up, rocking a bit in the process. Good gracious that movement didn't help the situation at all. She could tell he felt the same. He gently pushed against her. Reflex or intentional, she couldn't tell, though his gaze was dark with a sharp edge of desire.

She placed her hands on his chest. He grabbed her wrist with his free left hand and pushed against her again. Symphony's eyes slid closed. "Please…" she breathed, "Please hold that thought." She pleaded with him, but couldn't help rocking onto him once more.

"You sure?" He asked, grabbing her hip through her robe.

She stilled his hand with her own. "Yes. Since you brought it up, with your bedroom confessions. I have one of my own." His eyes were on her opened robe and cotton pink camisole. Her nipples responded to his unspoken call. They jutted out as if clambering for his attention. She was quite proud of her breasts. They were perky and large enough to get a handful, but not so large as to cause too much attention to herself. Although, they had Kyle's complete attention now.

"Kyle." Her voice was soft but demanded his attention.

"Tell me." He said, refocusing on her face.

"You mentioned that you didn't do casual flings."

"Yes."

"Well…"

"Yes?"

"That's all I've allowed myself to be involved in."

He moved his hand back behind his head again and bunched his brows together. "Yea?"

She could tell he was getting the wrong idea.

"Not that I casually sleep around, but the men I've been involved with, have been just that…"

"Just what?"

"Men I've slept with. I've only been in one relationship."

"Terry?"

She didn't want to be talking about Terry Phoenix while literally having Kyle pressed between her thighs.

"Yes."

"So…the other men?"

She shrugged her shoulders. "Maintenance."

The word came out so matter-of-factly that he chuckled.

"Maintenance?"

"Yes." Her face was serious.

"Random men?" He frowned.

"No. They were men that knew what the score was. That our arrangement was simply physical." He didn't say anything. Just looked at her. "This is very awkward." She announced, quietly. He was half-tied to the bed and she was straddling him.

"Not to me." He adjusted his head on the pillow and the horn from a large vessel passing by could be heard. "So, are we talking a lot of men? And what happened to them?"

She exhaled with frustration. This was turning into a mood killer. "No, not a lot of men. There were three besides Terry. I broke things off with the last guy about eight months ago. They were not just random fucks if that's what you're thinking. I'm very careful with my body and my heart. That's why the three didn't last. Because they wanted more. I didn't."

"So what do you want with me?"

She'd finally been honest with herself, so she would be honest with him. "I don't know."

He blinked at her, but his face remained impassive. "No?"

"No."

"Well what do you know?"

"I know that there's something about you that I can't shake…and to be honest, I don't want to." One side of his mouth quirked up. She continued, "I want to see where this goes. I want you to be the man who moves me."

"I can do that."

She wondered if he really could and would. "And FYI, I'm on the pill and have regular check-ups."

"Well, I haven't been with a woman in more than a year and have had my exit physical from the Army a short while ago, and checked out well."

"Is the confession booth closed?" She asked.

"It's open at your convenience."

With that being said and knowing that their talk had also cleared her question about what to do with her lack of condom situation. She slowly slid along his body planting kisses along his torso and shoulders.

"May we begin again?" She asked between kisses.

"Please."

She moved his hand from the back of his head and found the scarf to tie him to the headboard.

"Ready?" She asked.

"For whatever you got and want."

"Whatever?"

"Whatever." He stated confidently. "What do you want?"

"I want it all."

"You got it."

And this man, this man that she wanted to move her, wanted to be the one to bring her from darkness to the light, was beneath her. She would make him want to give all and she would give her all in turn. Currently, all she had to offer was physical, the rest would be a process.

She took his mouth and tasted fresh desire, a reflection, she was sure, of her own.

"Are you going to blindfold me, too?"

"No. I want you to get two blue eyes full."

"I plan to." He looked up at both his hands tied to the headboard. "Do your worst, Ms. James."

Still straddling him, Symphony pulled of the robe and tossed it to the side, lifted her camisole and dangled it between her fingers before brushing it across his face. He tried to grab at it with his teeth. She tossed it to the side as well.

"Oh, Baby…I plan to do my best."

She flung the covers away from them and took in his gray boxer briefs that shielded his thick rod. She could see the outline of it and couldn't wait until she freed him, so she didn't.

Symphony

Symphony eased off Kyle resting on her knees. She looked up his body to find his eyes waiting and yes, wanting as well. Her fingers slipped underneath the waistband and then slowly pulled down his underwear, careful not to catch his throbbing member. She tossed them and they landed in the pile of her discarded clothes.

He was free, hard, and oh so inviting. His penis was much lighter in color than the rest of him and could easily be used as a mold for women's self-pleasuring toys, she thought.

She wanted to take her time and lick him like a Popsicle, but she'd promised to ride him like a wild stallion. She couldn't help it though, before she climbed atop him, she let her tongue take a leisurely stroll from the base of him to his perfect head. She paid special attention to the ridge that shaped the top.

Symphony looked up at him. His soundless mouth was parted slightly and he was tugging unconsciously at his bindings. His hips thrust towards her and she let her lips envelop him. She couldn't take him all in, but she made love to him with her mouth for a few strokes before releasing him with a satisfied smack and then climbed onto him.

Symphony's clit screamed as she glided up and down against him. She leaned over, placing her hands on his chest and just let her slick flower tease him mercilessly. His moans were like a sweet sonata, masking her own and he wasn't even inside of her yet.

"Baby, I've got to touch you. These are going to kill me." He pulled at his hands. "I thought I could take it, but not this time. Not our first time. I need to feel you...touch you." His face was so earnest and voice filled with need. "We'll play this game later, but now..." She didn't let him finish. She pushed forward crawling up his body. The moment her sex left his, she felt such a sense of loss. Quickly, she untied him and scooted back. The crown of his erection met deliciously at the entrance of her backdoor. The sliver of wicked sensations surprised and peaked her curiosity, but before she could fantasize about it, she felt his hands burn and possess her.

They turned quickly into a mass of tangled limbs. Her breath caught as he flipped her onto her back. He took first, one nipple into his mouth and then the other and back again as if he didn't know which one deserved the most attention. Her hands dug into his hair and she wanted to beg him not to stop.

How had her seduction taken such a turn?

Kyle's lips sparked an internal ignition. Her body, her entire body roared to life in a way it had never before. There was no urge to put a stop to it—to bring this whirling tornado under control. She wanted its fierce strength, its heights and spans, she wanted its gravity defining chaos, and yes, she would even welcome the destruction, if that's what she had to sacrifice in order to experience this dynamic combustion of sexual energy and desire.

He kissed her everywhere, like he couldn't get enough and she didn't want him to. Hanging off the edge of reality, dangling just above exquisite surrender, he flipped her onto her stomach and covered her. The weight of him made her feel safe. His pulse steadied her. Burying his face in her neck, she inhaled the heady mixture of soap and raw possessiveness. Her arms spread out wildly grabbing at the sweet anticipation of pleasure-filled need. He lifted off her. She frowned at the disconnection. She turned back to look at him and found him just staring at her body.

She took care of herself. Owning a bakery could be detrimental to the figure so she worked out regularly, mostly taking kickboxing classes.

"You're so gorgeous. You have such great lines." He touched her shoulders and made a "V" along her back. How could something so simple make her damn near break apart? Her legs spread and the sound they made against the sheets could have very well been a mating call.

"You're not so bad yourself."

He smiled, leaned over and kissed the dimples above her bottom. He caressed each check then dipped his hand between her thighs to explore her petals.

"You're so wet."

"Yes." She breathed. "For you."

Kyle gritted his teeth and groaned. Without ceremony are any other priming, with her lying on her stomach, he brought his body down over hers again and entered her seemingly in one smooth motion. They both voiced their pleasure. She knew it would not take long for them to both climax. Her body vibrated as liquid heat slid luxuriously through her. She felt full. His warm breath caressed her neck as he pumped in and out of her. She felt so connected to him and met him thrust for thrust.

Somehow, she felt herself on her knees and she was on all fours pushing down into his lap. Kyle grabbed her ponytail, bringing her lips up to his and when his tongue entered her mouth, she burst apart in a zillion speckles of white light. The orgasm was so sudden and turbulent; she could not move—could not do anything but listen to the echoes of his name being flung into the room from her magnificent scream.

What happened?

What the hell happened?

Never.

Never in her life had the earth shifted beneath her during sex. Kyle's arm beneath her breasts were the only thing supporting her from crumbling to the bed.

Piece by piece the empty spaces of the life she was supposed to have was coming into view.

This man moved her.

Chapter 18

Symphony's sore muscles were tangible proof that the allergy attack following the bee sting left no lasting effects on Kyle. She couldn't help the smile that mingled with the quiet dawn while Kyle slept soundly as she watched Saturday emerge into existence. Steam from her coffee warmed her nose and she snuggled into the cushions. For years, she'd gotten up before the crack to bake, so she'd slipped from the warmth of Kyle and gotten up and baked.

"You must never want me to leave." She heard Kyle's sleep laden voice announce. Looking over her shoulder, she peeked up at him and then turned back to her coffee after she saw him take a shark-sized bite from a piece of the coffee cake she'd left out on the counter.

With her back still to him she asked, "What is it with you and coffee?" She turned to him then held up her cup. "Do you have a vendetta against its consumption?"

He grinned and strolled towards her wearing only his boxers. "Yes. It represents mornings that are too early to be seen in person."

"Not an early riser, are you?"

"Not by choice."

"But I do enjoy waking up to you." He gave her a soft kiss on her perturbed lips, nipped her earlobe, and whispered, "That, I can get used to."

"Me too." The confession didn't surprise her. She'd long since surrendered to the fact that she wanted to explore the idea of a fresh start with Kyle.

He sat next to her and she instinctively pulled her legs in and snuggled into him, careful not to spill her coffee. Remembering their night full of wild passion, warmth filled her and it had nothing to do with the coffee she held or the summer heat.

Kyle popped the last bit of cake into his mouth and stroked her side through her favorite pink cotton pajamas. The warm breeze kissed them both. She wondered how the catering job went last night and decided she would call Ian when she thought he was done with the morning prep. Symphony was surprised by the lack of anxiety she had about leaving her business in the hands of another.

"What shall we do today?"

"Well, I'm going to drink my cup of coffee and enjoy the sunrise and then I will go inside, call Ian at the bakery, brush my teeth to get rid of coffee breath, and wait for you to get back in bed with me."

Symphony

He said nothing, just settled into their comfortable position and they both waited for the happy ending that would begin their morning.

"I don't think it's a good idea, Alex."

"And why not? You're going to let someone from your past keep you from having a good time now; plus, I want you to meet my best friend Candice."

"I don't want to be a party crasher."

"Girl, this is the perfect opportunity to meet the other side of your island and Ethan and Sophia would love to have you. C'mon, Symphony. You know you want to come." And she did. She sighed into the phone. "Bring Kyle with you." I'd love to meet the guy that put a spark in you so quickly."

"Alex." She whined. She really did want to go and she wanted to get to know Candice and Sophia as well. Still, was it really a good idea to be there with Terry?

"I'm not taking no for an answer, Symphony. So get your butt in gear. If you need someone to go shopping with, we're all game."

And game they were. Not only did she get to meet Candice and Sophia, she got to know Gloria and

Alex even better. She couldn't remember having such a great time shopping.

"Dang, Symphony, you and Alex could pass for sisters. You two, may want to shake your family trees to see if there are some duplicates."

"Oh, hush Soph." You're always trying to start trouble.

"So, is Kyle coming with you to the party tonight, Sym?" It was Gloria who'd taken to calling her the shortened name Aunt Helen had always called her as a girl.

"Yes."

They were sitting at the same deli she and Alex visited the day before. They had the best turkey sandwiches, she thought. All eyes turned to her when Gloria asked about Kyle.

"So, what actually happened between you two?" Sophia blurted out the question everyone wanted to know. Symphony knew who she was referring to and felt she could trust these women. She wanted them to be friends.

"Nothing really. We had a thing in college, he went to do his thing, and I stayed to do mine." She shrugged her shoulders. "That's about the gist of it."

"But you wanted things to be different?" It was Candice who'd asked the question that Symphony wasn't quite sure how to answer.

"We knew what the deal was going in."

"Are you over him?" Candice's quiet question fell onto the table and stared up at her with flashing lights.

"Yes." The answer came out too quickly. The ladies looked everywhere, but at her. "I know what you're thinking, but I'm over him."

Sophia leaned across the table and said pointedly, "It doesn't matter if you're over him or not, when he sees you in that dress, more than his eyes are going to pop out."

They all exploded into raucous laughter. Symphony was looking forward to Kyle seeing her in and peeling her out of the sexy blue number, she purchased for the wedding reception.

She'd enjoyed meeting all the women and getting to know them. Together they turned out to be a pretty talented bunch. The tiny newlywed, Sophia, taught Latin dances to the stars. She had a studio in New York and now one in Boston where she also split her time volunteering at a school for the arts. She and Ethan married six months ago, but because of their hectic schedules and the insistence of the other

Phoenix women, were now just having their reception. She'd explained to Symphony that they'd gotten married without all the fanfare, because they were in a hurry to adopt a little girl. With all the paperwork and legalities done with the adoption of Bridgett, their new daughter, they decided to relent and have a small reception at Dixon and Gloria's home.

Candice, with her legs for days, the hue of rich coffee, used to run an art studio and was an accomplished artist herself. Gloria recently retired as an office manager for the Phoenix's Fortune 500 business, and still did it remotely to a certain degree. She didn't look anywhere near her mid-fifties. She also found that Gloria had a bit of a fetish for heels.

"Symphony, do any restaurants feature your desserts?" Gloria asked her while the others chatted about an event they were planning later in the year.

"A couple, but mostly my business is directly from the bakery or catering jobs."

"What's the deal with that guy Cooper trying to strong-arm you into selling his clients your recipes?" This question caused all eyes to focus on her.

"What guy?" All the other ladies asked in unison. The indignation in their voices, stirred something in Symphony. She'd never had a group of friends champion her before. Their response was warming. She really, really liked them.

"Cooper Read. The snake."

"What's he doing?" Alex asked her, sitting up putting on her lawyer face. "Has he threatened you?"

Symphony sat back in her seat, exhausted with having to deal with it all. "He's been trying to get me to sell a recipe to a frozen food company in Louisiana."

"Which one?" She asked frowning.

"Fox Foods."

"Dale Hemmingworth." Alex stated, flatly.

"You know him?" Symphony asked raising her brows. She was surprised that Alex knew the CEO of the company.

"I know of him. I studied a few of his company's court cases while in law school."

"Really?"

"Yea, remember I told you I went to school in New Orleans."

"What were the cases about?"

"There were several, but there're two that were pretty noteworthy. One was a suit against them for employee safety violations, which they lost. And the other…" she said, while pulling out her phone, "was a suit against them for recipe copyright infringement."

Symphony

Symphony's head throbbed. "Who won?"

"Fox Foods."

Symphony dropped her head in her hands. Alex reached over and patted her forearm. With the phone to her ear she whispered, "I'll take care of it." She held up a finger and asked for Sloan Channing. They all looked at Alex wondering who she was calling and why. When she mentioned the name Sloan Channing, Candice smiled and nodded her head. Candice caught Symphony's eye and whispered, "Don't worry."

How could she not.

"Yes...on Daddy's letter head." Symphony heard Alex say. "Symphony James. Yes... Cease and desist immediately...yea...yadda yadda...and sign my name, Alexandra Wyatt Phoenix...Ok...Thanks, Sloan." She clicked off the phone and looked at Symphony. "I assure you that Fox Foods will not bother you again."

Symphony's mouth was agape. Symphony had not known Alex long, but knew without question that she would not hear from Fox Foods again.

"Why...why would you do that for me?"

"Why not?" Alex tucked her phone back into her small leather bag.

"Because you don't even know me."

"Sure I do. We're friends, aren't we?"
Symphony nodded, not trusting herself to speak. "I know you're a wonderful person and I know that Terry Phoenix was a fool to let you go. I also know that I can't wait until tonight when I see the look on his face when he finally realizes it."

Chapter 19

"You're breathtaking. If I wasn't so vain I would keep you locked up here in the tower, but I want everyone to see that I'm with such a hottie!" Kyle stood just inside the door gawking at her.

Symphony twirled for him. Her newfound friends had talked her into this dress. The tank silk chiffon dress was a rich true blue, with thin straps and a draped back that fell to just above her backside. It just barely covered all the pertinent parts of her, but somehow the fabric made it elegant instead of trashy. The color, she chose, because it matched Kyle's eyes. The strappy silver shoes with touches of bling, added another flare of class to her outfit. She felt sexy and a little daring, though she was a little nervous about the evening. "Thank you, Sir. I feel kinda hot." She beamed at him. "Ready? We're going to take the boat over."

"I wanted to talk to you before we left."

Her forehead creased. "Ok." Her voice was hesitant. She led him to the breakfast table. "Do we need to sit?"

"Yes, we better, because you're in jeopardy of not making it to the party if you keep standing there.

But before anything, this is for you." He leaned down and placed a not so chaste kiss on her lips.

His kiss left her a bit dizzy. He was in jeopardy himself, standing there dazzlingly handsome, crisp and fresh in his light tan suit, pristine white shirt with no tie. His hair was pushed back behind his ears, more handsome than any man had a right to be.

She wiped the edges of her lips to clean up her smeared lip-gloss.

"Please, sit." She waved to a chair. He first went to her seat and pulled out the chair for her. They sat there like they were waiting for the beginning of an intimate dinner. "Well?" She asked.

He ran a hand through his hair. "You were right." He said.

"About?"

"I am a hypocrite."

His head tilted to one side as if weighing out what to say. She waited.

"The other day…" he began. "The other day when you accused me of being a hypocrite you were right." He tapped his finger on the table. "I go around telling people they should be happy with the life they have and here I am running from mine." He stood up and walked away from the table. He stopped and turned back to her. "I own a photography studio…Well, it was my dad's but he's retired now and he's passed it to me." She wondered why he was telling her all of this. "I know you're wondering why I'm telling you all of this, but I wanted you to know that I heard you."

"Ok."

He slid both hands through his hair and held them behind his head. His eyes looked troubled.

What was he trying to say?

"I'm out of my element here, Symphony."

"Meaning?"

"Meaning, you've got me turned inside out."

"I do?" For some reason his statement surprised her.

"Yes. Last night I told you I don't do casual relationships and you said that that's all you do." He stared at her waiting for confirmation of her statement, but she merely looked at him. He walked back to his chair and placed a hand on the back. "Your silence isn't filling me with baked cotton balls."

"Baked cotton balls?"

"Yea, baked cotton balls…warm and…"

"Fuzzy. I get it." He was such a goofball at times. "You said you wanted to talk, so I was letting you do it…I'm not sure what you want me to say." She shrugged. "Yes, that's what I said." She affirmed.

Symphony

"Symphony, I'm not crazy. I know that that guy has feelings for you."

She blinked rapidly, frowning. "What makes you say that?"

"Because after knowing you for two seconds, even when I was annoying you to no end, I was a goner." Symphony's eyes widened. "So, I know damn well that if you had a relationship with this guy, then he still has it bad for you. Something tells me that's why he's here…because he realized there's no way in hell that he should've let you go."

Alex had said the same thing earlier. Could that be the reason why he was here? Gloria told her that Terry was on his way to look for her.

Was Kyle jealous?

"Are you jealous?" She asked.

"I'm not jealous; I just want to know where I stand, before we go to this party and I stake a claim without a right to do so."

The edge of her lips quirked into a grin. "You want to claim me?"

"Completely."

"For how long?"

"For as long as you let me."

"You're right…All I know is relationships without any emotional ties." Kyle's shoulders slumped. "But, yes, you may claim me if I may do so in return."

His pleased grin warmed her. "Yes you may. And because I want to stake my claim on you, I wanted you to know that when I get back to Daytona, I'm going to do my best to salvage my life and stop letting demons of my past plague me." He reached and extended his hand to her. She took it and he pulled her into him. "One more kiss before you can reapply your lip gloss."

And kiss her, he did.

The soft pressure of his hand on her lower back filled her with anticipation for the end of the evening. "We better go." She whispered, her head resting on his chest.

"Ok." He breathed, but made no attempt to move. Her phone rang, startling them both. Reluctantly, she moved to grab her small silver bag off the table and fished out her phone. She didn't recognize the number. "Hello?" No answer. "Hello...hello?" The line went dead. Symphony looked up at Kyle, "That was strange."

"Maybe it was a wrong number."

"I guess." She gave him a soft kiss. "Come on, Kyle Dean."

Symphony

"Is that where the party is?" Kyle asked looking up in wide-eyed surprise.

"I guess." Symphony answered him, mirroring Kyle's surprise. "Alex said the reception would be on her boat…" She turned to Kyle who was still staring up at the huge yacht. "But I had no idea she and her husband owned this monstrosity. She told me they floated from place to place, but who knew she was speaking literally?" She looked back up at the massive sailboat and read the back. *The Phoenix.* Wow. The deck was lit with thousands of tiny white lights—a private sky. She couldn't wait to climb aboard.

"Symphony, my dear, welcome to Gwenda East." Dixon Phoenix took one of her hands in both of his, leaned in, and kissed her cheek. "We're so glad you could join us." He turned to Kyle and greeted him warmly, but she missed most of what he'd said. Mr. Phoenix was a good looking man. A really good looking man.

He matched Kyle in height, wore his gray slacks and white dress shirt like he just fell off the cover of a men's fashion magazine. From what she'd gathered from Alex, Dixon was in his sixties. His salt and pepper hair only intensified his mature allure.

Heat, she was sure, was pinking her cheeks. Gloria greeted Kyle just as warmly. She was stunning as usual, in a soft pink, flowy all in one pantsuit. The color accentuated her rich coloring.

The Phoenix's led them to an area where a photographer was set up for souvenir shots. "Come, take a picture now before your hair dies in this humidity." Gloria suggested.

The Phoenix stood like a sentinel in the background. A perfect backdrop.

"Canon five D, mark three?" Kyle asked the photographer.

The photographer squinted his eyes at Kyle and regarded him as if he was some kind of weird phenomenon. "Yea." He replied slowly.

"You prefer it better than the Nikon?"

Forgetting his earlier apprehension, the photographer patted the camera like a dear friend, "Ah, it's pretty much like comparing apples to apples. The only real difference in this one and the Nikon D750 is just the way they fit in your palms." He stuck out a hand to Kyle. "Gus Taylor. You a studio photographer or are you more out in the field?"

Kyle studied the camera a minute more. He touched it like it was fine porcelain and then walked behind it and looked through the lens. Symphony stuck her head in his line of vision and waved playfully. "Field." He said, looking at Symphony with a smile playing across his features and then back at Gus. "I was a combat photographer for a while and now I run a studio, but most of my work are action shots of all varieties."

"What lens do you use?"

"I have several, but the Canon EF 300 millimeter F two point eight…" They soon became background noise to Symphony. Seeing, touching, and talking about the cameras gave Kyle life. He lit up like a car lot on a big sale evening.

Symphony had no idea what they were talking about, but the sparkle in Kyle's eyes was bright and optimistic. They took their picture and walked with Gloria and Dixon onto The Phoenix. Sophia and Ethan, waited to greet them. Ethan was as handsome and charming as all of his Phoenix relatives.

They also met Alex and Candice's husbands Joshua and Landon. All of the Phoenix men had a strong resemblance, tall, very handsome, and had the same compelling smile. Kyle, however, was just as handsome in his own right, maybe even more so.

The massive sailboat was a nautical fairytale. Men and women dressed in white coats carried all manner of h'orderves and champagne. In addition, there was a bar stocked with anything else they wanted to drink.

Symphony stood at the rail looking over the water. A light fog was rolling in. Even with the music playing in the background and chattering of the thirty or forty guests, it seemed to be the most peaceful moment she'd experienced in a long time.

"You look beautiful tonight, Symphony." The voice she knew so well, traveled down the length of her exposed neck and back. Her lids slid closed and she turned to face him.

"Hello, Terry." Her dress fluttered in the breezed and she restrained herself from holding it down. She was self-conscious of its length, but instead she lifted her chin and tried to will the frantic beat of her heart. Over his shoulder she saw Kyle talking with Dixon Phoenix and then glance over at her and Terry.

"How are you?" He asked way too casually.

She turned her eyes to Terry. "I'm fine, and you?"

"I'm not doing so well."

She turned to look back out over the water. "I'm sorry to hear that." She said into the soft breeze.

"Yesterday, I asked you if you were in love with him."

"His name is Kyle." She said, turning back to him.

"Do you, Symphony...Do you love him?" She gave him a pointed look. "Kyle...do you love Kyle?" He corrected with a hint of sarcasm.

"Why is that any of your business, Terry?"

"It's my business, because I want you back, Symphony and I can't very well do that if you're in love with another guy. But if what you have going on with him, isn't that serious... I have a chance."

A short chuckle burst from her, though she saw no humor in what he'd said.

The audacity.

"And you think that all you have to do is simply say what you want and *poof*..." she threw her hands in the air, "just like that you'll get it?"

"Anything worth having is worth fighting for?"

"Wrong answer, Dude." She saw Kyle walking towards them. "We have nothing more to talk about. Your fight is six years too late!" She hissed, trying to keep her voice low.

"Forgive me for leaving you alone so long." Kyle stated as he placed an arm around Symphony's waist. Automatically she smiled up at him.

Why did she feel guilty?

"She wasn't alone." Terry stated with an edge of annoyance.

"Hi, I'm Kyle Dean; I don't believe we've met." Kyle said, extending his hand to Terry. "Thank you for keeping the prettiest girl at the party company."

"It was my pleasure." Terry responded gripping Kyle's hand firmly.

"Oh, I'm sure it was." He said with a smile that didn't reach his eyes. "You're the cousin of Landon, Joshua, and Ethan?"

"Yes." Terry said, not providing any other information. "Symphony and I went to college together."

"Yes, she mentioned that."

Terry looked at her, his eyes almost sad. She'd looked in those eyes so many times. So many times they could speak to each other without saying a word.

"Where did you go to school, Kyle?" He asked peeling his gaze from her. She was relieved at first. The heat of them was uncomfortable. But then she was pissed, because Terry was questioning Kyle about school like he'd attended Yale or Harvard, when in fact, he'd attended a school that she was sure most people had never heard of.

"My college experience was not typical. I went to college in between tours to Iraq. The University of West Florida."

Symphony missed the rest of the dick-measuring contest, because she was pulled away by Alex and Candice, to get a personal tour of the yacht. She reached back for Kyle. "I'm sure Kyle would love to see it too." She said looking back at him.

"Joshua will take the guys to show them all the nuts and bolts he had specifically placed." Candice and Alex laughed as if there was some sort of running joke she was missing. "I'll be back, Babe." She called out to him as the women ushered her away and the look on his face told her he was pleased by the term of endearment. A melancholy frown played across Terry's features.

Chapter 20

"I felt like you needed rescuing?" Alex whispered conspiringly. "He wants you back, doesn't he?"

"Oh God, Alex, why does life have to be so darn complicated?"

"Is it?"

"A week ago my life was orderly and uncomplicated."

"So what's complicated?"

Symphony shrugged feeling like she was ten again.

They went down a steep stairway, more like a ladder, which was a bit precarious in their heels, so they pulled them off and went down. The space opened up to a spacious dining area, bar, and very comfortable sitting area, decked out with every amenity imaginable. Symphony was awestruck. Her mouth fell open in wide-eyed astonishment. "Wow, Alex, this is gorgeous."

"We love it."

"Do you live aboard?"

"Yes, we live onboard, many months out of the year, but we have homes in Louisiana, Boston, as well as Bermuda."

"Wow." She couldn't help saying again. There clearly was much more to Alex and Joshua than she knew. She knew nothing about this life. It was also one of the reasons she knew she and Terry couldn't pursue a relationship. He lived and mingled with an entirely different class of people. She looked from Alex to Candice. These ladies lived in Terry's world, but had been nothing, but kind to her. Even more than that, they'd been the friends she'd never had. What if her apprehensions were unfounded?

"Come, let's have some girl talk." Alex gestured and led them to the plush seating area. It was far larger than her spacious living room. "He wants you back, doesn't he?" She asked again.

"That's what he says."

Candice's mouth dropped open. "He just came out and told you that?" She asked.

"Pretty much…he asked if I was in love with Kyle. He claims he needed to know that, because if I wasn't then apparently there isn't anything stopping him from trying to get me back."

"Do you?" Alex and Candice probed in unison.

208

They all chuckled, though like earlier, when Terry had said it, she didn't really find any humor in the situation.

"I've just met the man."

Candice and Alex gave each other knowing looks. Candice leaned back against the arm of the sofa, crossed her long legs, and said, "Neither of us," she began, motioning between her and Alex, "had known our husbands long before we were in love."

"I like Kyle a lot, and I really want to explore a relationship with him. He has such a wonderful spirit and it doesn't hurt that he's fine as all get out!"

"Well that's enough, for now." Alex pitched in, laughing. "And Terry says, if you aren't in love then he thinks he still has a shot?"

Symphony frowned. "Yea."

Candice leaned forward. "Maybe he thinks you're still in love with him."

"He can think what he wants. but right now, I'm interested in moving forward and not looking backwards." She was looking forward to doing that with Kyle. It also pissed her off that now, all of a sudden, he couldn't live without her.

And as if Alex could read her mind, she asked, "What if Terry would've wanted to start a life with you right after you two finished college?" Symphony shifted in her seat and looked everywhere but at Alex. She seemed so much older than the other two, but they were all about the same age.

"You're like a mother hen." Symphony shot at her, but couldn't hold the smile. Alex's gaze didn't waiver. Her brow began to inch up her forehead. She wanted an answer. "Ok…Ok…put your guns away." Symphony crossed her legs and felt the cool air on the underside of her upper thigh. "I don't know…He didn't ask."

"But what if he had? Did you love him enough to give your relationship a chance?"

"I don't know…I think so."

"So, maybe you need to figure out if you really don't love him or if you do and you're just pissed and hurt because he didn't try harder to keep your relationship alive."

"I take it back." Symphony confessed, rolling her eyes. Candice and Alex both frowned in confusion. "I only *thought* I wanted girlfriends…I thought you were supposed to be on *my* side?"

"We are." Alex said, standing. "Come on. I'm sure the guys are wondering what we're up to and getting worried that we're plotting to take over the world or something." They both hugged Symphony who was even more confused than ever.

Was Alex correct? Was she still in love with Terry?

No.

She decided who she was or was not in love with. Didn't she?

When they emerged from below decks some of the guests were leaving and she didn't see Kyle or Terry, for that matter, anywhere. She hoped they weren't off somewhere duking it out over her. That thought gave her a twinge of giddiness—to think two men may want to fight over her. Her aunt had been the only one who'd ever done that in her life. She thought again about Alex's question and wondered again, if she'd been distraught over Terry not fighting for her.

She stood at the rails again. Now, big wet cotton balls of fog hung low and thick. She couldn't see very far in front of her.

"Excuse me ma'am, may I take your photo for the album?" Symphony turned wondering what her hair looked like by now. Surely, frizzy from the evening heat and fog. Standing in front of her with a triumphant sinister smile on his thin lips, was Cooper Read.

"What the hell are you doing here, Read?" Apparently, he hadn't gotten the memo to cease and desist. "And how did you know I was here?" She looked around. "How did you get onboard?"

"Never mind that. I'm here. That's all that matters." He was standing much too close to her. She could smell his cheap cologne. It burned her nose.

"You're looking especially lovely tonight, Symphony James." He reached for her arm and she jerked herself away, only to feel the rail against her back.

"There's nowhere to run." He said. "And why would you want to?"

Symphony looked around and saw none of the Phoenix's nor Kyle. Where the hell had they all gone?

"You're going to give me those recipes, you bitch." Something within her told her this man was not only unscrupulous, but also dangerous. Fear raced through her limbs, but her face remained impassive. "I've worked too hard and made too many promises for this deal not to go through."

What was he talking about?

"You're going to give me the recipes." He said again, "And sign the contract."

"Are you out of your fucking mind?" the fog was beginning to obscure the deck of the yacht. She could barely make out the sail masts above her. "You better let me go or this ass whipping that is planned for you will be intensely worse." She demanded with confidence. She was suddenly grateful for the kickboxing lessons her aunt insisted she take, and for her continued training during her frequent gym visits.

His laugh was brittle and mocking. Good. Let him believe she was all bravado. Unsuspecting victims fell easier.

He shoved a manila envelope into her chest. "If you don't, I'll expose you." The envelope wasn't very heavy, but its weight and stiffness told her that it was not the contract. "Open it!" He growled.

She did. There were pictures of her in various stages of dress and a few of her having sex. The man's face was hidden in the first two pictures, but there was a picture of his ass in the next. Eric! She would know that behind anywhere. From the background of the hotel room, it was the last time they'd been together.

How dare he!

She stared up at Cooper who grinned with sadistic triumph. She cocked her head to the side, anger rolling through her. "What?"

"If you don't want those pictures leaked, I suggest you sign this contract." He shoved the document in her face that she hadn't noticed before.

"Again, I ask, are you out of your fucking mind?" She placed a hand on her hip and stood with her legs braced apart. "Who the hell cares about those pictures? I'm no priest or politician. I'm a baker. Who cares if they see me naked? It may actually bring me more business."

His eyes narrowed with realization that his blackmail was not working.

"But I know one thing," she continued. "You won't be able to see out of one or both or your eyes in just a few minutes."

Cooper Read was so preoccupied with getting a rise out of her; he hadn't realized she'd slipped out of her shoes. When he did, it was because the heel of her foot was coming across his head. Before he could react to the blow, another was coming from the other side. "I've been on my own a very long time, you asshole!" She screamed at him. "You don't think I know how to take care of myself?"

When he fell, she saw he had a black pistol tucked in his waistband. He had a gun. The bastard had a gun. What had he planned on doing with it? Did he think he could force her into doing what he wanted? The pictures and gun let her know that, that's exactly what he'd planned to do.

Cooper Read, lay unmoving at first on the damp deck of *The Phoenix*, and then she heard him groan. Only then, did she realize she'd better yell for help, unsure if he would try to get up and fight back or what. It didn't take long for the remaining guests, including Kyle, to come running.

At least she hadn't fainted, Symphony thought as she sipped at the glass of wine Gloria gave her to calm her nerves. It was difficult, because she was still shaking from the encounter. Kyle had gone out to make sure the police would be taking Cooper to jail. They'd already spoken to Symphony and she'd relayed the details of what had happened. Somehow he'd mingled with the guests and come aboard the boat. The police asked her if she'd received any strange phone calls lately. She remembered the few times the phone rang and no one answered. Apparently, it was a new technique for criminals to hack into and track cell phones to find the location of their victims.

The entire time she spoke to the police, she kept looking at Kyle, wondering how he really felt about what had happened. Would he think she came with too much baggage? That question was quickly waylaid when he pulled her into his arms after the questioning.

"Are you ok?" He kept asking her. "You sure?"

She found herself missing his company now and wished he was still there to hold her.

Symphony

"What's this all about?" She watched the envelope slide across the table before she looked up at Terry and found that his glare matched the accusation in his tone.

"It's none of your business, Terry." She said, picking up the envelope and placing it in her lap. She'd wondered where they'd gone. She'd told the police they must've fallen overboard, but here they were.

She looked up at him and the heartbreak and disappointment reflected in his dark eyes slapped her. The sting of it caused her to flinch and look away. She didn't think she could stand it if Kyle looked at her that way. Those pictures made her look seedy and cheap.

"I just want to make sure you're ok, Symphony." He sat next to her, his words no longer flanked with the indictment of his previous tone. They were soft and concerned.

"I'm fine." She snapped. Her reply stung him, she was sure, but she didn't feel like having to explain herself, least of all to him.

"I love you, Symphony, and six years ago I was too young and pig headed to realize I needed to fight for you." He rubbed his hand on the back of his neck. "That last night…" Why the hell did he have to bring that up? All she could see was him at the door and her wanting to express her love in a way he wouldn't forget. Apparently he hadn't forgotten and he knew she hadn't either when he gave her a look that spoke to her carefully guarded heart.

"I'm sorry, Terry, but it's too late for us."

"It's never too late to right a wrong, Symphony."

"I can't have this conversation right now, Terry. I'm not sure if it's even worth having."

"Is he what you want, Symphony? Kyle, I mean? I heard Alex say that you just met him."

Kyle walked into view with purposeful strides, face tight as he took in Terry's intense look and posture. "Are you ready, Baby?" He asked Symphony.

Symphony turned to Terry and said pointedly, "Yes," and then back to Kyle, "I'm ready." She gathered her shoes by her feet, the envelope from her lap, and stood. She looked over at Terry who was standing as well. "Good bye, Terry. Take care of yourself." Kyle placed a possessive arm around her waist and guided her away.

Terry grabbed her arm at the elbow. "Symphony, I won't make the same mistake twice." Terry announced with certainty. She and Kyle turned to him. The nerve of him, she thought.

Symphony snatch her arm and opened her mouth to speak, but Kyle stepped forward. She didn't know him well enough to know what his reaction to Terry's revelation would be.

Both men took measure of each other. Kyle rubbed his chin and pushed his hand in his pocket. All Symphony could do was stand back and watch the soap opera unfold.

"If you haven't noticed, Phoenix, I'm the man in her life right now. Trust me; I don't blame you for wanting her back. I would be kicking myself too, if I'd walked away from her, but the simple fact is, you did. What you had is over. And I'm not just saying this because I want it to be, I'm saying this, because that's what Symphony has told me and her actions confirms it. So, if you still want to throw down the gauntlet, then be prepared, Sir, I'll be more than happy to pick it up."

A surge of satisfaction flooded her with Kyle's statement. He was letting Terry know that in his fight to win her back, he was going to be that much more determined to hold on to her.

Terry seemed to look at Kyle in a completely new light. His eyes widened a fraction and his confidant stance annoyed her, because it was six years too late.

"If you two are done with your pissing contest…" she stated looking between the two of them. "Or will you call each other out for a duel next?" She turned and walked off, completely exhausted by the entire day.

"I'm ready to go home." She needed her kitchen back. She needed normalcy.

In the morning, she would leave Gwenda Island and go back to Florida.

Chapter 21

"Good morning, Marylyn." Symphony said cheerily as she walked into the bakery, Monday morning during peak. She'd planned on arriving at her usual time to help with the prep, but Kyle convinced her that she'd enjoy sleeping in with him much more.

And she had.

Symphony wasn't surprised that Kyle joined her on her flight back to Florida, even after she insisted that he continue his sabbatical like he'd set out to do. He was still worried about Cooper Read and Fox Foods harassing her, although Alex was filing an official complaint against them. She'd taken on the job as Symphony's attorney.

Marylyn stood frozen with tongs in her hand and a donut on the end of it.

A donut!

She didn't sell donuts. They were too…ordinary. Symphony looked in the display case and noticed there were a couple of trays of them and looked around to notice several people eating them. Marylyn's eyes went wide and terror attacked her features as she watched Symphony examine the recent changes.

Symphony

Symphony frowned when she saw Marylyn's expression. Did she do that to people, make them terrified of her? "Good morning, Stephanie." Symphony smiled pleasantly and Stephanie and Marylyn looked at her like she was an alien.

She guessed, to them, she was.

"Hey, Baby. Did you think I would leave without stopping in at my favorite place?" She didn't have to turn around to know it was Kyle; plus, he'd grabbed her from behind and snuggled into her neck. She knew his touch, his scent, and the familiar sensations his voice produced.

Marylyn dropped the donut and tongs she was holding and the entire bakery fell into a hush. Symphony squirmed out of his grasp and giggled. "I was hoping you would come by." She grabbed his hand, "Come on, let's go to my office."

He looked longingly at the pastry case. "Do you have something sweet in there?"

She gave him a wicked grin, "I'll let you be the judge." Ignoring the stares from every pair of eyes in the place she walked behind the counter and through the swinging door that separated them from her kitchen.

Symphony walked into the kitchen. Ricco was putting pastries on a rack and Ian looked as if he was boxing up desserts for a catering order. Symphony handed Kyle a plate. "Here pick out what you like while I talk to Ian." Kyle pulled in a fist pump like he was at a rock concert. Symphony giggled and turned to Ian who was staring at her not unlike Marylyn and Stephanie had. "Ian," she waved at Ricco, "Ian…Ricco, this is Kyle Dean; he's a lunatic fan and a friend."

They both nodded at him, "Hey guys!" He yelled and turned his attention back to the pastries.

"Will you be ok for a minute?" She asked Kyle. He waved her off. She giggled again and Ian didn't know where to look. She noticed the new mixer and patted it. "How's the new mixer?" Before he answered, she waved him to follow her, "Come on, catch me up on the place, Ian." He followed her to her office, which looked exactly liked she'd left it. "Well…how's everything?" She sat behind her desk, "I noticed donuts out front."

Ian shifted from one foot to the other, "Yes, Ma'am." He lifted his chin, back ramrod straight. "Many customers requested them. They were coming here for pastries and going to the Donut Den for donuts to bring to work, school, and such." Had she been so selfish that she'd ignored the needs of her customers?

"I see." Her face was aloof which was probably the reason that spurred his defensiveness.

"They are anything but ordinary." He stated with a bit of pride.

Symphony tried to hide her smile. "Yes, I noticed. They make quite an impressive display."

"We've sold nearly as many of them each morning as some of the pastries."

Her brows raised. "Yea?"

"Yes, Ma'am."

"It looks like you've done a fine job, Ian." She looked up at him standing there and sighed. "Will you please take a seat?" He sat, though his legs seemed exceptionally long while seated. "I have a proposition for you." He was silent. "I would like for you to be the store manager?"

Kyle suddenly appeared in the doorway. "These donuts are like your pastries…but…in a donut!" He exclaimed. "Oh my God! I can die now." He turned and ventured back into the kitchen, presumably to get more.

Symphony chuckled and looked to Ian. "Seems you have a fan."

"No, Ma'am…They're your recipes, I just put them in another shape."

"So…?" She prodded him back to her original question.

"We don't have a manager."

"Yes, I know. That's why I would like for you to be the manager. I'll hire someone to help Ricco, but I would like for you to run the bakery."

"Run the bakery?" The astonishment on his face was endearing. "But that's what you do."

"Yes and I'm tired." It suddenly occurred to her that he may not want the responsibility. "It's a bit of responsibility, I know, so I'll understand if you don't want it."

He shot out of his seat. "Yes, I want it!" His voice uncharacteristically animated. "It will be an honor."

"There'll be a significant raise in pay, of course." He simply nodded his head "Oh, by the way, we shouldn't be hearing from Fox Foods or Cooper Read, again. Ian sat back down while she explained all that transpired when she was away.

He was appalled by Read's intention to blackmail her, though she'd left out the parts about the pictures. Speaking of which, she hadn't yet talked to Kyle about them. Thinking of Kyle, she thought maybe they could spend the day together like tourists in St. Augustine. Maybe going to the lighthouse or the wax museum—fun stuff that she'd never thought about doing until now.

Symphony would have a meeting with the rest of the staff later to tell them that Ian was now the manager. It should be an easy transition for him, since he'd been running the entire bakery since she'd left nearly a week ago.

She found Kyle sitting cn one of the stools placed near the small stainless counters in the back, watching Ricco box dozens of pastries. He was practically drooling. "I'm getting jealous." She whispered next to his ear. He spun her around and placed her in his lap. She heard Ricco gasp. "I don't think you look at me like that, even when I'm naked," she whispered.

"I do, but you're usually asleep. Don't want you to think I'm some kind of perv." He was about to kiss her, when he realized they had an audience. Ian quickly cleared his throat and turned back to what he was doing.

Ian's gait and posture was noticeably confident, now. He was a godsend. She would make sure to pay and treat him well, so she wouldn't lose him.

"Do you two need my help for anything?" Ian and Ricco looked at each other and then back at

Symphony, like the question was some sort of booby trap.

Ian gave them an easy knowing smile. "We're fine, Symphony. You two go on and enjoy yourselves." It was the first time she remembered him using her given name. It made her feel good that he was more comfortable with her now.

"Let me get caught up in my office and then how about we spend the day in St. Augustine pretending to be tourists?" Symphony asked him with arms still thrown around his neck.

"Sounds good to me. May I join you or do you need some privacy?"

"Join me, please." She leaned over so only he could hear, "You're supposed to let me know if I have anything sweet in there."

He rapidly raised and lowered his brows. She jumped off his lap before he tried to carry her in there. Symphony saw two faces looking through the window on the door to the restaurant. Waving quickly as she ran to her office, the faces disappeared. Symphony knew they all probably thought she was crazy, but she didn't care. She felt good and she was happy.

Walking around to her desk she heard the click of the lock on the door. She lifted suspicious eyes to his darkening ones. "You wouldn't dare?" The accusation came out weak and nonthreatening.

"Oh, but darling, I would." He said as he quietly strode towards her. Each step sent a tremor through her. "And I believe you secretly want me to…Don't you, Symphony James?" He walked around the desk to stand in front of her. She could feel the heat from his body mingle with hers. He leaned down and placed panty-melting kisses on her neck and along the "V" of her t-shirt. Her eyes slid shut and all she could do was feel the sensual pulses he was creating in her. Sweet seductive need stacked within her. "Don't you?" He breathed against her skin.

"Yes." She voiced in a suffocated whisper, because he was literally taking her breath away.

His hand breached the boundaries of the bottom of her t-shirt and ventured north. Every portion of her flesh his hands met, begged to be his. And she knew. She knew like she knew the sun would continue to set, with or without her, that she wanted Kyle Dean to take her on her desk, in her chair. She didn't give a dame where, as long as he did. "Please, Kyle." The plea was insistent and he wasted no time stripping off her shirt, unsnapping her bra, and feeding greedily on her nipples. She could feel them berry into hard pebbles as his tongue worshiped them, one by one.

227

Symphony

"Kiss me." She managed to say. She had to get him off her breast or she would come apart. Her folds begged to be explored and oh how she loved when he played with the entrance to her sex. He pulled off her black and white checkered chef pants and she stood there before him clad in lacy black panties.

"My... my... my..., don't you look delicious." He praised her. "But do you taste as sweet as you look?" He pushed her into her leather office chair and his smoldering gaze sent a jolt of excitable pleasure through her. "We won't need these." The feeling of the lace traveling down her legs was an exquisite prologue to what she knew was coming. Kyle scooted her to the edge of the chair, dropped to his knees, and threw her legs over his shoulders. All she could see was the top of his blonde head dipping down to sample her dessert.

The first pass of his tongue on her swollen button had her on the threshold of heated ecstasy. When he used his finger to penetrate and toy with her entrance, she unexpectedly came apart. It was so fast, but oh so exquisite. Kyle's touch was potent and pleasurably provocative. Never had she come apart so easily.

Symphony slammed her hand over her mouth to keep from screaming out for the entire bakery to hear, but she didn't have time to even worry about

228

being heard. With her orgasm still raining down on her, he pulled her up, turned her around, bent her over, and filled her, almost in one motion.

When had he removed his shorts?

Surely, she wouldn't be able to come for a second time, but relished the feel of him inside of her anyway. Soon, she began to climb the mountain of another orgasm.

Oh my...

Kyle slammed into her. His strokes carnal and wild, with each push and glorious pull, leaving her wanting him deeper, harder, faster. She loved the feel of her bottom slapping into his front. Each smack of skin on skin sounded too loud, but she didn't care. This was her office and if she wanted to get freaky in it, then she would damn well do it.

At least that's how she felt at the moment with her naked behind tooted in the air with seven inches of velvety soft, rigid pleasure, stroking her so expertly.

Kyle held her hips firmly. His large hands digging into her flesh, branding her, claiming her, making her his. She wanted to be all those things and at that very moment she was his, completely his.

Symphony knew when Kyle was nearing his peak. Her name crawled from the hollows of his throat and lit the fuse that raced to detonate her own explosion. The pieces of her that hadn't shattered against the walls of her office, felt his frantic thrusts before he completely buried himself into her. His essence erupted from him and blended with her own. In that moment their souls spiraled in unison, dancing to a beat that belonged only to them. As she held on to the arms of her chair, he groaned and half collapsed onto her back. The weight of him, moved and grounded her—grounded them... together.

She no longer felt damaged—unwanted.

Piece by piece, Kyle was putting her back together. All the fragments that she'd either thought were broken or buried beneath hurt and rejection, he was piecing into a picture that made sense—a picture that was whole and desired.

Never ever had she thought about having sex in her office. It was the most exhilarating experience of her life.

"Kyle Dean, you're going to be the death of me."

"My sentiments exactly, Ms. James." He said through rapid breathing that mirrored her own.

Chapter 22

At the end of the week as they were leaving Symphony's, Kyle cradled a box of pastries like he was the Virgin Mary and it was the sleeping baby Jesus. Symphony just shook her head, secretly pleased with his love of her baked goods.

"What's up with your staff?" Kyle asked her. "They were like soulless, gawking…"

"Idiots?" She finished for him.

"Well…" He squinted and rocked his head from side to side. "Not Ricco and Ian…they seem halfway normal, but those two in the front." He rotated his index finger around his ear and whistled like a bird in a cuckoo clock.

"They probably think aliens have abducted me and swapped my body with another Earthling who has an actual heart. They'll probably worship you forever for finally getting me what they think I needed."

"And what's that?"

Stone-faced she said, "Laid."

"Let's take my car. We'll get yours later." Kyle said, chuckling. He pulled his keys from his pocket with his free hand and nodded towards one of those crossover SUVs people were driving more and more these days. "I'm over there. The parking lot was crowded when I arrived this morning." He'd surprised her and showed up as soon as they'd opened.

The black Lexus seemed too serious and formal for her beach bum.

Her beach bum.

The idea strolled slowly around in her mind, sat down with legs crossed, and made itself comfortable there.

Before Symphony climbed in the car, she looked up at the sky. The blue of it startled her. When was the last time she saw a blue sky in the morning? It was always dark when she got to work and late afternoon when she left.

When was the last time the sky demanded something of her? No clouds obstructed its view and it was absolutely breathtaking that just beyond the azure, the universe stretched forever.

It was overwhelming. She pulled the hair tie from her head and shook her wild mane free. Holding her face up to the sun, she let herself be kissed by the beautiful Florida sky.

She hated to get in the car, but did anyway.

Kyle frowned as she climbed in. "You ok?"

"Yea...Just noticing what a beautiful day it is."

"Beautiful indeed." He replied, not taking his eyes from her. Eventually, he started the car and backed out of the space when he got a chance. The lot was still pretty crowded. "What? They don't think you have a heart?"

She sighed, turning to him. "I guess I haven't given them much reason to believe that I do." She turned to the window and looked up at the sky again, remembering what he'd said on the plane. "Everyone thinks I'm a bitch...remember."

"Just goes to show you that you can't judge a book by its cover." She could hear the remorse in his tone.

Her shoulders rose and fell with her sad sigh. "I guess I've never given them reason to want to open the book."

"Ouch...that bad?"

She nodded, "unfortunately."

"No wonder they seemed so freaked out."

"Yea."

Neither said anything.

"Hey!" Symphony tapped his arm. "Let's ride down the coast."

"Anything for you, Beautiful."

"Anything?"

"Absolutely." His smile filled her with a piece of the sky.

She bit her bottom lip trying to decide the best way to ask him what she wanted. When she hadn't responded, he turned to look at her. Taking in the seriousness of her features, his smile faded and his forehead creased.

"What?"

"Will you show me your studio?"

He gripped the wheel and stared straight ahead. She could tell he missed it just from the things he'd pointed out to her everywhere, while they were flying, and just by they way he described colors to her. He'd even asked about her menu and who'd taken the pictures for her boards.

Kyle glanced at her, but she couldn't tell what he was thinking. Life was too short not to do the things you loved, she thought. She'd loved baking, but she'd also missed out on some of the little enjoyments in life. And the little things are what she now knew, made up the larger things. He needed that camera to fulfill a need he had within himself.

Symphony watched Kyle's arms relax and he settled more into the seat. She tried to keep her face expressionless, but it was difficult; she really wanted him to share his studio with her.

"On one condition." He said, finally.

"Anything."

Kyle glanced at her and turned back to watching the road, but the smirk on his face told her she'd left herself wide open.

"Ohhh…the possibilities." He teased.

"So, you'll show me…really, Kyle?" She beamed like a kid with a new toy.

"Yes."

She leaned over the console and placed a wet smack on his cheek. The car swerved a bit. He hadn't been expecting the kiss.

"And in return?" She probed.

"Spend the day on the beach with me."

"Absolutely! Just bring me somewhere I can get a suit." She felt full of sunshine and blue sky. Spending the day on the beach sounded wonderful.

"I can do that."

Symphony cocked a smile at him as she placed her hand on his thigh. "So…" Her voice suddenly seductive and low. "Kyle Dean…have you ever been given a French kiss…here," her hand covered his manhood, "while you were driving?"

Damn near choking on his surprise from her words, he swerved the vehicle onto the shoulder and it rattled from the grooves that separates the driving lane and the emergency lane.

"No." He choked out.

"No?"

He pinned her with a look from the corner of his eye.

"And no, I haven't." She answered his unspoken question. "It can be a first for us both...I was thinking that maybe we can declare this day an official Kyle and Symphony holiday and I'd like to do things that I've never done."

"I'm definitely game!" He showed her by holding her hand in place on his growing erection.

"Well then..." she wiggled her brows, "let the games begin."

Symphony was in complete control of the first game. She wanted to be outlandish and spontaneous. She was thankful the console wasn't too high and the armrest lifted. She moved the shoulder strap of her seatbelt and without ceremony or any pretense in being shy, she unzipped Kyle's shorts, gently searched for the opening in his boxer briefs, and pulled him free. She looked up at him.

"In order to play this game and win, you have to keep your eyes on the road, you must not swerve the car, or pull over…and you have to keep your hands on the wheel."

Slivers of anticipation made her tingle. She was so turned on by the thought of pleasing him. Her hand was already gently stroking the length of him and with each stroke, searing arousal electrified the confines of the of the SUV. Kyle's breath hitched.

"I'm pretty sure I'm going to lose this game…" he hissed through gritted teeth, "or win…hell…I don't know which…It all seems like a win for me."

Her lips on him clipped his words. She unsnapped the belt to reach him better. "Don't kill us, I have to unsnap the belt."

Symphony's hair fell around her head like a golden fortress shielding her actions from his view, but the low moan that he tried to contain, let her know that she was probably going to kill them both.

She released him, moved her hair from her eyes, and looked up at him.

"On second thought, pull over." And immediately she felt the car move over and come to a stop.

He picked up a lock of her hair and the tips of his fingers skirted over her shoulder.

"Uh unhh… hands on the wheel." Her command sent his hand straight to the wheel. The highway wasn't too crowded, though she felt the car rock a few times from the passing vehicles. His windows were tented pretty well, so there wasn't much chance that others could really tell what they were up to. And without further comments, questions, or concerns, she made love to him with an intimacy she'd never granted another.

Symphony let his moans and squirming, guide her. With each hitch in his breath, her tongue got a private lesson in pleasure. She was granted expert tutelage with every sound the syllables her name made rolling off his lips. And after a short while, the perfect "o" his mouth formed when he reached his peak, told her she'd learned and applied her lessons well.

Chapter 23

A few blocks from the beach, in the middle of other store fronts, stood a three story red brick building with six large windows, three on each of the two upper floors. There was a small sign above the double doors on the first floor that read, "Dean Photography," in fancy script.

Her eyes rounded, looking up at the structure while he parked, she exclaimed, "This is it?"

He nodded.

"This is your photography studio?"

"Yes." He stated again, passively.

"It's huge!"

"Yes."

Still looking up at the studio, she was shocked by its size. She'd been expecting a tiny building with room enough for a lobby and a small area where families sat and posed for shots they would regret in ten years.

"Come in. Let me show you around."

They unsnapped their seatbelts and she searched his face for any signs of apprehension, but there were none. He came around to her side to open the glove compartment. He pulled out a set of keys and

239

turned to her, leveling darkening eyes at her and the unquenched need thrumming between her thighs sang loudly with awakening. The car game had left them both extremely horny. It was evident in the prolonged glances, the seductive touches, and it was definitely evident from the wet panties that she wanted to get out of.

Before arriving at the studio, he'd stopped at a shop nearby that sold a variety of swim suits. She'd jumped out, grabbed a bikini instead of a one piece, because it was a day to do things she'd never done. She also picked up a cheap pair of flip flops and shorts. She held the bag in her hand as he paralyzed her brown eyes. A slow secret smile, that she completely understood spread across his face.

"Ready to go in?" She asked.

"Mmm, hmmm." He murmured pressing his mouth against hers in a kiss that stole all her senses. She felt his erection press against her thigh and oh how she wanted this man.

This man and no other.

A car horn startled them into awareness and he led her to the door. Inside, was an open space full of various lighting equipment and backdrops. It was massive, but before she could try to make sense of any of it. She heard the ding of an elevator that she hadn't noticed. The doors opened and he pulled her inside. Before they closed, he had her against the wall with his mouth on hers hungrily, making it impossible to ask any questions. Kyle shoved his hands into her hair, deepened the kiss, and torched her from the bottom of her feet to the top of her head. With urgency, his touch branded her again and she welcomed every mark.

She vaguely heard the rattle of the elevator door closing. It jolted them a little as it lifted. Kyle took that as a green light to pull down her chef pants and panties. She kicked off her sneakers. She was thankful the pants had a drawstring. It made it easier for him to get her out of them. Before returning to her she saw him stick a key in the panel. Once her feet were free and her bottoms were kicked to the side, he lifted her and she wrapped herself around him like he was her lifeline to keep her from drowning.

Back braced by the wall of the elevator he fumbled for only a second before finding her slick slit and entered her. She pulsed around him and knew nothing in life could feel as good as Kyle Dean filling her.

The elevator clattered to a stop and she instinctively tensed and looked towards the door.

"Don't worry, the door won't open." She relaxed, her body charged by the thrill of having sex in an elevator and from the push and pull of pure pleasure drumming through her. She felt weightless, lifted by the stupor of desire spiraling through her. Higher and higher she climbed until she erupted like a volcano.

"Kyle!" She gasped as the damn broke and sensations she couldn't name, caused her release to spill all over him. It was the trigger that initiated him to stiffen and follow in her wake.

"Symphony!" Her name being torn from his lips with such passion, sent her over the edge again. Surprise, elation, and exquisite relief crippled her. She was boneless and completely at his mercy.

She was a flake of ash floating carelessly to the ground without worry as to where it will land.

She would've agreed to just about anything at that moment. All she could do was be held against the wall and feel their pulses of aftershock in complete sync.

The third floor, she was surprised to learn, was his apartment. It was the length and width of the building, which made it much larger than her home on the golf course. Everything was either very white or monochrome. Framed black and white pictures were the focal points in every room.

Symphony

The kitchen was all stainless steel and white marble. It was simply beautiful. Wrapped in a huge fluffy white towel, she slid her hand along the marble island and longed to make something on it.

"Do you cook?"

"Not at all." He said, pulling on another t-shirt.

They'd showered together and made love under the warm spray of water cascading down on them. Another first for her. She quickly realized that she wasn't as experienced as she thought she was. She'd done things with Kyle that she'd never even thought about. She'd read about them in romance novels, but just thought they were outlandish acts that romance writers came up with to make the love scenes more interesting.

"Are you going to put your suit on now." He'd already put on his trunks and looked the epitome of a young gorgeous surfer.

"Yes." She pulled it from the bag. "Like it?" She held up the the simple white strips of fabric.

His tongue fell out of his mouth. "May I photograph you in it." His face suddenly serious.

The question stabbed her newly found bravado. She remembered the pictures Cooper Read tried to blackmail her with. She'd never been a prude, but she'd felt violated by them, because they were done without her permission and used with the intention of making them perverse.

Kyle was not Cooper Read.

He had been completely honest with her since they'd met and she had no reason to believe he would use the photos as leverage against her. And like she'd told Read, who the hell cared anyway?

"Sure." Her answer was confident even if she felt apprehensive about what his camera would reveal.

"Get changed and I'll set up downstairs. I'll send the elevator back up for you.

"Ok." She said, almost shyly.

Symphony changed into the bikini and padded over in bare feet to the elevator. She took the shaky ride down that was way scarier than her ride up to his apartment. She grinned thinking about the activity that had distracted her. The elevator jolted to a stop and the door creaked open.

With her head down adjusting a string on her bikini bottom, she stepped off the elevator and walked right into a man who was not Kyle.

"Ahhhh!" She screamed and was about to flip straight into kickboxing-ninja-mode when Kyle ran out.

"Dad!"

Symphony

Dad?

She looked at the man who with wide eyes, was just as startled as she was, and was taking in her state of undress. She quickly jumped behind Kyle to hide herself. Kyle's dad who was an older copy of his son, peeked over Kyle's shoulder with a mischievous twinkle in his eye.

"Dad?" Kyle asked, confused. "What are you doing here?"

With a smile on his face he brought his eyes to Kyle. "I was just checking the mail. I saw your wagon and thought I'd come in and say hi."

Kyle sighed. "It's not a wagon, Dad."

"Well whatever you call it." He looked over at Symphony again. "Who you got with you, Son?"

"This is Symphony James, Dad. Symphony, this is my dad, Warren Dean."

Mortified, Symphony peeked over Kyle's shoulder and wiggled her fingers in a wave.

Mr. Dean muttered her name over and over and looked at her again. "You aren't Harold James's daughter are you?"

Symphony stiffened and just stared at him. Another first. She hadn't heard her father's name mentioned aloud since he'd tried to contact her after she'd opened Symphony's. Apparently, he'd been in prison and somehow saw the notice about her new business. The officials at the prison told her it was a common occurrence for inmates to randomly choose contact information from those notices in hopes to solicit a pen pal or love interest. In her case, he was soliciting money.

He claimed she owed him. For what, she had no idea, but she'd written him back and told him that she didn't know anyone by the name of Harold James and requested he no longer contact her. She'd also followed up with the prison to notify them that she was being harassed by one of their prisoners. They told her that she wouldn't be contacted by him anymore, and she hadn't heard from him since.

Symphony stared at Mr. Dean. How was it possible for him to know the man who was supposed to have fathered and raised her?

Chapter 24

All in.

That's how she would describe her and Kyle's relationship so far. From the moment she'd given him one of her pastries on the plane, she'd been all in with him. With her conversation, with her time, with her body. Symphony was all in with the way she expressed herself with and through him.

Was she all in with her heart?

Two weeks of nonstop Kyle.

It was air. He was air.

Pure oxygen that filled her lungs with bird songs flying underneath a pristine blue sky. He was her pot of gold. Her golden dream that gave her the moon just because he said it was the only thing that could match her smile.

She loved his parents. It was still weird that Kyle's father knew her dad. They'd gone to high school together and had met up again shortly after Symphony was born. She'd told Mr. Dean in as few words as possible that she hadn't seen him since she was four and didn't know what had become of him.

The pictures Kyle had taken of her that first day in his studio had come out great. They were simple and

247

bold at the same time. Because there were no backgrounds or props, just her in her white suit. She'd stood out like a piece of artwork. He'd enlarged a few and framed them, which made her a little self-conscious and delighted when she looked at them hanging in the bedroom of his apartment.

She looked hot and sophisticated. Kyle was a genius with that camera and made her feel comfortable in front of it. She knew he was finally getting away from his ghosts of the past and looking forward to the future and what he could do with his business. He'd even talked to his Army buddy, Harris and made plans to visit him soon.

Symphony was happy, simply because she allowed herself to be.

Ian was running the bakery and she didn't micromanage him. She trusted her judgment for making him manager and she trusted his judgment and him.

Before, she'd worked six days a week from open to close, but now she worked four days a week for about four to six hours a day—long enough to still leave the magic in her baked goods, but also leaving her time for herself.

Like now.

Symphony

The laundry and cleaning could not wait another day. She was out of her usual routine and that was ok, but the laundry had piled while she'd played with Kyle the past two weeks.

Symphony was transferring a load from the washer to the dryer when the doorbell rang. Gloria had called her earlier to let her know some documents that related to her properties were being forwarded to her and would be arriving today. She tossed the clothes in and hurried to the door, dressed in a t-shirt and yellow yoga pants.

"Coming!" She called out.

Yanking open the door, she stopped short—frozen. It was not the currier with the documents.

"Are you going to let me in, Symphony?"

There were so many words coming to mind that they kept crashing into each other and she couldn't put them into a coherent sentence.

"Symphony?"

Silence.

"How?" Finally, a word spoken aloud. She found a few more along with anger, making them jagged and hard. "How dare you?" She spat.

"How dare I what?"

"What are you doing here?" She snapped at him. "How do you even know where I live?"

Symphony

"May I come in?"

"No, Terry, you can't!"

"I drove here from Charleston."

Her head cocked to the side and the look she shot at him told him she didn't give a damn.

He seemed to enjoy watching the fire leap from her features and that infuriated her even more. Folding her arms over her chest was the only thing she could do to keep from slapping that smug smile of his off his face. Closing her eyes and shaking her head, Symphony wished by some miracle that he would just disappear and transport himself back to the past where he belonged.

Unfinished business.

He was unfinished business and deep down she knew she had to lay her past to rest or it may continue to show up on her doorstep unannounced.

She let out a short hostile breath before stepping aside to let him in. Kyle had been the only man in her home. Terry Phoenix standing in the middle of her living room bigger than life, seemed like an intrusion—a betrayal.

What would he say if he knew Terry was here with her while he was driving his mom to the doctor in Orlando? Would she tell him?

Symphony

Of course she would. There was no reason to lie and Kyle would understand. Symphony inwardly groaned. How could *he* understand when she didn't?

"You may as well sit down." She waved to the seating options in her living room, which wasn't much. There was the big comfy chair and ottoman she loved and the sofa and loveseat. "Do you want anything to drink…water, iced tea…wine?" Her voice empty and flat. Hospitality was ingrained in her. Kyle had beer in the fridge, but she'd be damned before she offered his beer to Terry. That seemed more of a breach of loyalty than him being in her house.

"I'll have a glass of wine, if you don't mind." He said, sitting on the ottoman.

She kept glancing up at him as she got the glasses and a bottle she'd just opened the night before. He was looking around either at the starkness of the place or just because he didn't know what to do with his eyes while he waited.

She reached in the fridge to pull out the bottle.

"It's a chilled Riesling, if that's ok."

"Perfect." His voice coming from just the other the side of the refrigerator door, caused her to stand up too quickly. She hit her head on the freezer handle.

"Shit!"

"I'm sorry, I didn't mean to startle you." His voice laced with more humor than concern. "I just came to ask if you needed any help."

Help, she needed, yes, but not with the wine. She rubbed the top of her head. What she needed was him back on the other side of the room. He took the bottle from her hand and poured them each a glass in the two she had waiting on the counter. She picked up her glass quickly, trying not to let him see the trembling her double-crossing body displayed in her hands.

"A toast?"

"To what? We have nothing to toast."

"Sure we do." He said as he clinked glasses with her. "To…"

"…closing the door to the past." She said, just as he said, "…our future."

There eyes met. She saw something there that she didn't want to see.

Hope.

Symphony walked passed him and took a seat on the sofa. She placed the glass on the coffee table, needing to get a coaster, but didn't.

"You haven't lived here long?" He asked sitting on the ottoman again, across from her.

She frowned. "Why do you ask?"

Symphony

"Because it looks like you've just moved in. There aren't any trinkets lying about and you only have the clock on the wall."

He was right. Her off white walls were bare. It looked like she'd just moved in. Before, she'd been too busy to go shopping for house knickknacks, but found that she wanted to now. She'd been picking up a few things here and there for her bedroom, but not for any other area of her home. There was a place in Charleston that she wanted to return to, so she could by some things for her house.

"I've lived here for about three years."

He raised a brow. "Oh?"

She rolled her eyes, took more than a sip of her wine, and crossed her legs. It was crisp and cool, but did nothing to help her defend off his presence. Why was she so nervous?

"Well?" She finally asked, wanting to get on with their talk and with her life.

"You've never told me…but that last night you showed me." He put his glass down, stood, and sat next to her, their knees nearly touching. Her eyes followed his movements and his proximity to her was disconcerting. Just the mentioning of that night made her shift uneasily in her seat. "I want to hear you tell me that at one time you loved me."

He's finally learned how to get straight to the point, she thought.

It was not what she was expecting him to say and because she didn't, the truth popped out without restraint. "Yes." Symphony watched relief blossom in the illumination of his brown eyes and give life to the hope already driving his movements.

"Yes." He repeated the single word. A statement. A life summed up in three letters.

She could feel the single, softly spoken word grow bigger and bigger in front of her until she could feel herself being swallowed by it.

Yes. Yes. Yes...

Louder and louder she heard it like church bells alerting a town to disaster. She picked up her glass to keep from slamming her hands over her ears, to block out the sound and nearly spilled its contents. She couldn't look at him. She had to do something, but sit there. Quickly, she drank down the half glass and stood.

"I'm going to pour more." She felt his eyes on her back as she hurried to the kitchen, but really wanting to bolt from the room—from him...from the truth.

Symphony

She'd never said it and had only admitted it to herself after he was gone. Why hadn't she told him? Would things have been different?

She didn't see how they could've. He was still going to Boston and she was not. She had a bakery to open.

At one time she had loved this man enough to trust him with her heart. Was it he, or she who had betrayed that trust? Had she really trusted him with it if she had ended it prematurely?

Why hadn't it occurred to her that she could open her bakery somewhere else. All this time she'd blamed him for not fighting for her. The resentment, the regret, the pain...could it all have been her fault?

Symphony gripped the edge of the counter, standing in a patch of uncertainty, unable to keep the pain from wracking her body. She felt the tear slip off her cheek before she knew she was crying. Her face itched from the trail it left, but she couldn't move. She couldn't breathe.

She was stuck—rooted to the spot grasping for clarity that had been too transparent for her to see.

Symphony let him pull her hands free and engulf her into his arms. His sure hands rhythmically stroking her back was familiar, but not soothing. She felt as if her heart was breaking all over again.

Symphony

"Shhhh…shhh…" He crooned. "It's not your fault, Symphony."

His t-shirt felt soft against her face and he still wore the same cologne she'd loved. It reminded her of a warm fire and tangled limbs. For just a moment she allowed herself to remember. To remember what it felt like to be in love with Terry Phoenix. To remember what it felt like to have his smile directed at her. For just a moment she allowed herself to pretend that she'd never told him that it was over.

And then she remembered these were not the arms that she'd given permission to hold her. These were not the hands that knew exactly where to touch her and send her soaring. This was not the man who she'd allowed to claim her.

Symphony pushed away from Terry slapping the moisture from her face. "I…I can't."

"It's not too late for us, Symphony." He whispered.

She looked up into pleading eyes. "There's no us, Terry."

"You can't stand there and tell me that we have no connection. I know you felt it." He took a step towards her and she backed away. She shook her head.

"Symphony, I should've fought for you…I should've figured out a way for us to be together."

Symphony

She just looked at him before her eyes slid shut and she sighed deeply. "I didn't trust you enough to take care of my heart."

"Let's sit and talk."

She followed him back into the living area, but didn't really see what they had to talk about. They'd both made mistakes, it was in the past, and that was that.

He sat next to her on the sofa again. She would let him take the lead in the conversation, because she had no idea where to go. She didn't want to go back, she just wanted to go on with her life.

Terry grabbed her hands that were twisted nervously in her lap and she let him.

"Symphony, we still have a chance to start a life together. We still have a future…I love you and I can't believe that we're over. I can't believe that what we once shared can't be recovered." He kissed the palm of her hand. She felt like porcelain on the edge of an unstable table. She closed her eyes. "Six years ago we were too young to realize that our destiny's were in each other. Please, Symphony give us a chance."

His voice blanketed her in a whisper and swirled into blocks of ice that crashed hard against her.

What do you say to a man who thinks of you as their destiny?

"I can't…"

"Shhh…" He stood and pulled her up with him. "Think about it Symphony. You said you loved me. Think about how you felt that last night we were together." He leaned down to her ear. "Think about how good we can be together." He kissed her on the forehead and walked to the door. "You may have moved on, but has your heart?"

The evening glow came in when he opened the door. He turned to leave.

"Terry!" He turned back to face her. "How did you know my name that day in the library?"

"You told me in a dream." He said it so matter-a-factly that it couldn't be refuted.

A dream?

And then he was gone.

Regret.

She owned it. It was like a stolen work of art, priceless, exquisite, and useless besides the fact that it was in her possession. She could look at it, touch it. She could worry and wonder if she should have it. She could hide it away and hope no one finds it stowed behind the walls.

Chapter 25

Two Months Later

The day began and was coming to an end beautifully. Over the past two months they'd done all the things she never thought she wanted to do, like walking the boardwalk in Daytona, touring the haunted graveyards in St. Augustine, and they'd even driven to Orlando one weekend and visited a couple of the Disney parks. She had loved doing all those things with Kyle, except getting sick after riding Space Mountain. That she could've done without. But ever the gentleman, instead of being repulsed by her nearly puking all over his shoes, he'd been very attentive. They'd found a family restroom and he'd gone in with her to help clean her up.

Earlier, at the top of the lighthouse, in town, he'd taken lots of pictures with his camera of the two of them with the trees and water channels below. He'd even given an interview to Time Magazine a few days ago.

They'd walked around most of the day, enjoying some time on the beach. She was exhausted and a little queasy. Probably because she'd gobbled up everything in sight. She would have to hit the gym hard to make up for it.

They pulled up in front of her modest home. She never told Kyle that Terry had visited her here. There was no point. She was moving forward.

It was nearly dark. Sometimes she wished she lived closer to the heart of St. Augustine to be closer to her bakery, but was thankful to be away from all of the tourists. She'd left her car at the bakery where he'd surprised her that morning, again. It was becoming a habit.

Like the morning after her arrival from South Carolina, their day began with a hot rendezvous in her office. She'd had to create a new office area for Ian. Imagining him working at a desk that Kyle had made love to her on was too much to think about.

"We can get your car in the morning, or would you rather get it now?"

It was a foregone fact that he would be staying the night. They were never ready to part. She'd also spent several nights at his place.

"I'll just get it in the morning." He drove most of the time when they went places. "Plus, my seats aren't near as comfortable as these."

They got out and he grabbed all her packages from the back. The buzz of Symphony's cell phone interrupted her searching for her house key. She blinked and quickly scrambled to answer the call. "Alex?" She asked in a rush. Kyle looked over at her, both hands loaded with bags. Symphony looked again for the key and fished it out. "Hold on a sec, Alex, we're just coming in the house."

"We?" She questioned.

"Yes, and stop being so nosey." She opened the door and pointed to the sofa where Kyle could drop the bags. "What can I do for you?"

"I'm sorry to have to ask this of you, but I need you to fly to New Orleans."

"New Orleans?" Symphony looked at Kyle and frowned. His returning frown had the shadow of a question. "Why do you need me to go to New Orleans?" She asked into the phone.

"For a brief court appearance. Fox Foods is a Louisiana based company and most cases in that area ends up at the U.S. Fifth District Court..."

"Court?" She cut her off and lifted troubled eyes to Kyle again. "I thought everything was taken care of with your cease and desist letter."

"Well it would've been if Read hadn't taken things into his own hands and escalated a possible civil case into felonies."

Symphony

"But, I told everything to the police that night of the reception."

"I know, and I hate to have you go all the way to New Orleans, just to get your statement recorded"

She sighed into the phone. "I guess…if there isn't any other way around it."

"I'm not asking you to go to the electric chair, Symphony. Don't sound so glum. It's New Orleans for Pete's sake!" Symphony didn't say anything. "Plus, we'll get to hang out at one of my places…and maybe I'll get a chance to convince you to let us highlight some of your desserts at my restaurants."

Symphony was surprised by her last comment. In the past she would never have considered it, but Alex wasn't Fox Foods and wouldn't try to mass produce her desserts. She could possibly still make them at her bakery and have them shipped fresh. It may be expensive, but it could be done. Something to consider.

"When do you need me to be there?" Symphony asked.

"Well, I'm headed out tomorrow. If you could get there tomorrow or the next day, that'll be fine. Maybe you could spend some time with us in Baton Rouge…What do you think?"

"I'll check flights and get back to you in about an hour or so. Not sure about Baton Rouge, though, I'm in the process of breaking in a new assistant in the kitchen."

"Ok…well… I'll look forward to your call later." They both clicked off the line.

"Shit!" Kyle looked at her expectantly. She fell into her favorite chair and held her head in her hand. She just wanted all this crap to be over. "Alex needs me to go to New Orleans."

"How long have you been dealing with those bullies at Fox Foods before you kicked that dude's ass on Gwenda?"

"For at least six months."

"Are you going?" He walked over to her and scooted in next to her. "To New Orleans, I mean?"

"Doesn't look like I've much of a choice." She relaxed into him. "I just want all this mess behind me."

"Would you like for me to go with you?"

"I couldn't ask you to do that."

"You're not asking." He said nuzzling her neck. "*I'm* asking if you would like for me to go with you."

"I've enjoyed being with you these past couple of months, Kyle…"

263

Symphony

"I get it." He said and began pushing away to stand. "I don't want to smother you."

"I don't want you to either, and you're not." She turned to face him and placed her legs across his to keep him in place. "What I was going to say was…I've enjoyed being with you, but I don't want to make assumptions…I don't want to become an obligation."

"Are you kidding me?" He frowned and glanced up at her. He must've saw the sincerity in her face because his brows raised in surprise. "You're serious, aren't you?"

"Well yes, Kyle, we've only been seeing each other a short while. Why would I assume you would want to come with me?" She linked her hand in his. "Plus you're trying to get the studio up and running again." She knew he was itching to get back to his camera, just from all the fuss he'd made from their shots at the top of the lighthouse.

"I thought it would be obvious." He said kissing the tip of her nose. The playful kiss was like drinking sunshine. She really liked Kyle.

Giggling, "Well, it isn't to me."

"You're so square, Symphony Blaire James."

"Square must be your thing, Mr. Dean." She shifted on his lap. "What's your middle name?"

Symphony

"Why yes, Ma'am…square is my favorite shape." He tweaked her nose. "Believe it or not, my middle name is James." His brows danced, playfully. "You're my destiny; I can feel it."

She chose not to respond to his last words or the thrill and misery they evoked. They weren't so unlike what Terry had told her. "You're kidding." She chuckled, pushing thoughts of Terry as far away from her and Kyle as she could get him. Symphony rubbed her nose. "Were your parents a fan?"

"What do you think?"

"I think that for your name to be Kyle James Dean, then yes, they were more like fanatics."

"My dad is a macho type of guy. He didn't care for the name Kyle, but my mom had her heart set on it. So, my mom let him add James in there to beef it up." He cradled her in his arms and she was beginning to love her chair even more. He brushed his lips across hers and she couldn't think of another place she wanted to be at that very moment. "Of course, my only reason for wanting to go with you, is to give me an excuse to go to New Orleans…Duh!"

New Orleans with Kyle James Dean was suddenly beginning to have grand appeal and so were his lips just an eyelash away. She arrested them and it was like walking across a bridge to her soul. And there she found the essence of Kyle intertwined so completely that she knew.

Symphony knew with total clarity that she was on her way to falling deeply in love with Kyle Dean. He made it too easy; too easy to let him in. Nothing in her life had ever come easy. So, naturally, fear encased her. She just hoped that she wouldn't let her anxiety keep her from enjoying herself. And she dearly hoped that she didn't let her emotions turn her into an idiot.

The latter was her greatest fear.

Chapter 26

How had she lived twenty-eight years of her life without visiting this city? From the moment they stepped off the plan she felt like she'd been transplanted into a different world. The air sizzled with excitement and everywhere she saw posters and billboards for food that she couldn't wait to try.

"Have you ever been here?" Symphony asked Kyle as he drove towards downtown in their sporty red rental.

"Yea, some buddies and me came out here on leave for a couple of weeks when I turned twenty-one. Though I don't remember much of the visit."

"Why not?"

"The drinks were really cheap and we were really stupid."

She raised a brow. They were weaving through morning traffic and the Superdome was coming into view. She turned from the window and he waved an irresistibly devastating smirk at her. "Oh and I'm sure the ladies were falling like flies to that charm of yours," she said.

He took one hand from the steering wheel and grabbed his heart. Inflecting his words with a perfect

French accent, he said, "Do you think I'm charming, Mademoiselle James?"

"Working on your Creole?"

"There's no work involved and you didn't answer my question."

She leaned over and placed a kiss on his cheek. "Why yes, Mr. Dean, I think you're too charming for my own good." She replied, sounding like a perfect southern belle.

"I'm not sure if I should be offended or if that was a complement."

She simply smiled and looked out of the window again. This was only the second time she'd traveled anywhere with a man before—the first a complete disaster.

It was thrilling and a bit scary, especially since she was sure she was in love with him. This wasn't like Charleston; this time they were traveling with the intent of being together as a couple.

A couple.

She was part of a couple. She couldn't help the school-girl grin.

"Hey." She asked suddenly. "How old are you?" The fact that she was traveling with a man and she didn't even know how old he was made her question her sanity.

Symphony

"I turned thirty-one, yesterday."

Her head snapped towards him and her eyes and mouth flew open. "Are you shittin' me!"

He laughed out loud. "You have a potty mouth, Ms. James…but no, I'm not shittin' you."

"Why didn't you tell me?"

"Telling you wouldn't have made it any more perfect than it already was." His face softened and he glanced at her for a second before focusing back on the expressway. "It was a perfect birthday. I got exactly what I wanted."

And Symphony thought it had been a perfect day as well. She tucked her hair behind her ear, licked her lips, and smiled at him. "Happy Birthday, Baby."

Kyle gripped the wheel tightly. "Say it again."

"Happy Birthday."

"No…no, not that part."

The corners of her mouth lifted. "Baby." Her voice sounded like velvet even to her own ears.

Kyle shook all over with great exaggeration. "Who would've thought that a grown man would beg to be called Baby?" He said, apparently pleased by the endearment.

Kyle dropped Symphony at the front of the hotel where Alex suggested them to stay. It was also

Symphony

close to the courthouse. They'd decided to self-park so they wouldn't have to wait for their car if they decided they wanted to go somewhere. "I'll wait for you in the lobby while you park the car."

"Ok. See you in a few minutes."

The streets were all so narrow with "One Way" signs to complicate directions, so she knew it would be more than a few minutes for him to park. Maybe valet would've been better.

Symphony checked in at the front desk, got her keys, and waited for Kyle to meet her in the lobby. There were quite a few people moving around, but what really caught her eyes was the exquisite décor that totally contradicted with the Bohemian colors on the façade.

"I was hoping you would be alone, so we could talk some more."

She wanted to bang her head against the wall.

Terry Phoenix…again.

Symphony inhaled and let out a deep breath slowly and loud, making her annoyance quite clear.

"Why can't you seem to understand that there is nothing for us to talk about?" She snapped, angrily.

"That's my question as well." Kyle interjected as he walked upon them.

Symphony

Symphony, suddenly wondered if this was Alex's way of trying to get her and Terry back together, when just then, Alex and Joshua walked into the lobby.

"What the hell are you doing here?" Alex demanded of Terry, taking in the tightened jaws on all their faces.

Joshua scowled at him as well. "Damn it Terry, is this why you were asking so many questions last night?"

"This is none of your business, Josh." Terry stated coolly.

"The hell it isn't. You used me to get information about Symphony, so you could come here. This isn't the way, Cuz."

Symphony noticed that people were beginning to look their way. This was all Terry's fault. Joshua pulled Terry off to the side and Alex hooked her arm around Symphony's. "Walk with me to check in." They headed towards check-in. "Sorry I'm late, but I was cramping so badly when I got off the plane that we had to go to the drugstore to grab Midol…Mother Nature's torture."

Symphony froze and she could feel the blood draining slowly from her face. All of a sudden she heard a chorus of string instruments hit the wrong note.

Symphony

Her head buzzed like she was going to faint again and she was underwater and couldn't reach the surface.

Why hadn't she noticed?

Why hadn't she paid attention to the signs? The fatigue, the nausea, the sudden increase in her appetite. She'd noticed her pants seemed a little tighter, but she'd attributed it to all the junk she'd eaten lately.

But she was on the pill...

Her cycle had come like clockwork most of her life. Why hadn't she noticed that she hadn't had one in two months?

"Symphony, are you ok?" She felt Alex shake her gently.

No, she wasn't ok. She looked over at Kyle who was now walking towards them—his face painted with concern.

"Symphony!" Alex nearly shouted. She couldn't seem to release herself from the cloud of astonishment that she was most likely pregnant.

By this time, Terry and Joshua were also walking towards her and Alex.

Symphony used the pamphlet that incased the room keys to fan herself. "I'm ok." She couldn't say it was the heat, because it was a perfect fall day outside. The temperature was a perfect seventy degrees. Pretty cool for October in Louisiana. "Just a little dizzy from not eating breakfast."

Her eyes lifted to see the frown on Kyle's face when she told the lie. He was about to say something when...

"Kyle Dean, is that you?" The screechy female voice came from behind her and Kyle. They all turned to face the woman. Kyle blinked a few times frowning before recognition surfaced. He stiffened and paled. Symphony looked from him to the woman who was wearing fuchsia shorts that were way too small and too young for her pasty dimpled legs. The white halter top left no secret she wasn't wearing a bra.

"Is it really you, Kyle? She asked again, walking up to him.

Uneasiness began to settle in Symphony's belly and she willed herself not to throw up. Who was this woman and what was her relationship to Kyle?

Kyle looked at Symphony and then back at the woman. "Ummm...I..." He stuttered.

"It *is* you!" The woman launched herself at him. Symphony looked around at Alex, Joshua, and Terry, who seemed just as confused as she. Though, Terry's face held just a touch of smugness.

Kyle peeled the woman off of him. "Shelia?"

273

Symphony

Shelia looked around at their little entourage. "Isn't he the cutest?" She said, intimately stroking his arm. "Seems like you would know your own wife when you saw her."

All eyes were on Kyle. His were on Symphony.

Symphony couldn't believe her ears, her eyes, or the realization that she'd again been a fool to love.

"Is this your wife?" She couldn't even believe she was having to ask the question.

"Yes." He stated somberly.

Dear Diary,

Twice, love has led me astray. It will not happen again. It will not happen again. It will not happen again. It will not happen again.

Symphony

Kyle

The day of her aunt's service, Kyle had never been so overwhelmed by a woman in his life. Her grief caused pain to slice through him like nothing he'd ever felt.

When he'd met T.J. at the harbor where they'd first arrived in Charleston. T.J. told him that Symphony's aunt had died and that the services were scheduled for that day. He knew he had to be there and when he saw her smile of recognition, he knew she was glad to see him as well. Selfishness had led him there. If she'd needed comforting, he wanted to be the one to provide it for her.

There was something about this woman that moved him. When he saw her in the TSA line, the sadness in her eyes drew him to her. He'd wanted to hold her since that moment. He wanted to be the one who brightened her world. Why he felt that way, he didn't know, but it was immediate, overwhelming, and unyielding. He wanted Symphony James.

A perfect world is to be able to close, board, and barricade the windows to the past. He was learning

276

through very harsh lessons, that this is not a perfect world.

Because he'd found a beautiful light in Symphony, he'd finally been able to deal with the demons he'd met in Iraq, but now, he was faced with the past of his stupid youth.

Whose big idea had it been to spend two weeks in New Orleans, anyway?

Kyle sighed.

Did it even matter at this point?

All he knew was somehow he had to get Symphony to talk to him—to listen when he told her that he loved her and that what they'd shared is worth saving.

Terry

Not again. He was not leaving without Symphony. Six years ago he'd let his family dictate his life. Tell him where to work, where to live, who not to love.

Not again.

Yes, he'd probed his cousin and his wife for information about Symphony, but he had to. It had been two months since he'd held her, he'd seen the regret in her eyes, saw the tears from it. More than anything he wanted to take away the pain. He wanted her to tell him to stay.

Symphony told him that she'd loved him, and he'd bet every dime of the Phoenix empire that she still did. She just couldn't think clearly right now, because she had a distraction. And that's all he was—a distraction. That's all he could be, because she belonged to him. There was nothing against Dean personally and Terry was sure under different circumstances that he would probably like Kyle, but the man had his woman.

She was the woman in his dream.

Literally.

Symphony

A week before his high school graduation and adamantly against going to college or working in the family business, Terry thought it a great idea for his friends to take a road trip to Manhattan before they would all split up for the summer. He didn't remember much about that weekend, because there had been lots of drinking and marijuana.

One night he'd dreamed he was napping on the beach in Florida underneath the beams of a ninety-degree sun. "Hey…hey…dude! You better get up; you're going to burn."

He roused awake, squinted, and shielded his eyes from the brilliant sun. And then, there she was, blocking the light with her head. Her auburn hair framed her face like sunbeams and her t-shirt had been cut and fringed at the bottom. It read: Flagler college, across the front.

"Who are you?" He asked.

She smiled a smile that seemed so familiar.

"I'm Symphony."

"Maybe I'm the maestro?"

She rolled her eyes, "Clever…You better get up, you're burning."

He opened his eyes to find that his friends had piled as many blankets and clothes on him as they could find. It had been difficult to breathe and he was burning up.

The dream had been so real that he'd made plans to go to that school in Florida, the moment he returned to Boston.

Every now and then, he'd have a dream so vivid and real that it seemed like he'd lived it instead of just dreaming it. It was kind of like déjà vu, but more tangible. He had such a strong feeling about the dream of him on the beach, that he felt it was more like a glimpse of the future, rather than a sleeping fantasy.

So real, that he'd bet his future on it.

When he saw her that day at the library door, he knew it was destiny. She was his destiny. That, he was sure of. He must've been completely out of his mind to have left her.

Not again.

All he knew was somehow he had to get Symphony to talk to him—to listen when he told her that he loved her, that he'd never stopped, and what they once shared is worth saving.

It cost more than he'd anticipated. His meager funds were dwindling quickly, trying to keep up with that bitch, but he knew it would be worth it in the end. He stared at the box on the table, wondering just how he'd execute his plan.

"If Symphony James thinks she's seen the last of me, then she's sadly mistaken." He spoke aloud to the dirty walls in the small worn apartment. "No one disrespects me and just walks away."

He moved to the stark newspaper-covered window, pealed a piece away and peered onto the the dark streets, riddled with the rank taste and putrid smell of poverty, abuse, crime, and lost hope.

It was her fault he'd ended up here, in the toilet of this city.

Her fault, and she'll pay.

She. Will. Pay.

Symphony

Dear Reader,

Thank you as always for taking this journey with me. Symphony had been lying on the floor in the flour for way too long and it was time for me to get her out.

Symphony began as a short story that I wrote well before *The Pleasures Collection* was born. It was time to get to know her better and to find out why she seemed so broken and dark. Half-way through this novel, I realized that her story would take more telling than one book could hold.

I hope you have enjoyed getting to know our Symphony, Kyle, and Terry. Their story was not ready for an end, so I'm hoping you will forgive me for the cliffhanger and hold on for the final chapters of their story. This is a romance of course, so now the question is, who will end up together and what conflicts will they have to endure?

Joyful Reading,

Natasha Simmons
www.natasha-simmons.com